THE FIRST AND LAST MISTAKE

Remo was annoyed. After all this time, Chiun still demanded he prove his skills, even in such a simple matter as saving the Lincoln Memorial from terrorists.

"Ten seconds," the last remaining terrorist shouted. "If I do not push the button back down, we all die!"

Remo moved then, his hands like spearheads. He reached the man, slapped his hands apart, and in the split-second when the detonator hung in the air, Remo jammed the button down.

"Oh, shit!" Remo groaned. In an instant he realized three things. The terrorist had lied about the detonator. The explosives were about to go off. And there was nothing he could do to save the Lincoln Memorial, let alone himself.

"Run for it, Chiun!" Remo cried. "I blew it!"

The Destroyer

76

THE FINAL CRUSADE

Created by
WARREN MURPHY & RICHARD SAPIR

A SIGNET BOOK

SIGNET
Published by the Penguin Group
Penguin Books USA Inc., 375 Hudson Street,
New York, New York 10014, U.S.A.
Penguin Books Ltd, 27 Wrights Lane,
London W8 5TZ, England
Penguin Books Australia Ltd, Ringwood,
Victoria, Australia
Penguin Books Canada Ltd, 2801 John Street,
Markham, Ontario, Canada L3R 1B4
Penguin Books (N.Z.) Ltd, 182–190 Wairau Road,
Auckland 10, New Zealand

Penguin Books Ltd, Registered Offices:
Harmondsworth, Middlesex, England

First published by Signet, an imprint of New American Library, a division
of Penguin Books USA Inc.

First Printing, April, 1989
10 9 8 7 6 5 4 3

PUBLISHER'S NOTE
This is a work of fiction. Names, characters, places, and incidents either are
the product of the author's imagination or are used fictitiously, and any
resemblance to actual persons, living or dead, events, or locales is entirely
coincidental.

For Peter and Karen, and Brandon and Sheena. On the occasion of the first anniversary of their conversion to Sinanju.

Prologue

On the day the Ayatollah died, a rocket launched by the Mujahideen Khalq struck the square called Maydan Sepah, in the heart of Tehran, narrowly missing the shop of a wizened old rug merchant named Masood Attai.

When the dust cleared, Masood breathed a prayer to Allah. The prayer turned into a muttered imprecation when he noticed the lightninglike crack that had appeared on the rear wall. The portrait of the Ayatollah, which Masood had only an hour ago rehung with black crepe, lay on the floor, its glass front shattered.

He looked for the nail. It could not be found.

Masood walked out into the settling dust, pinched his flared old nostrils with cracked fingers against the smell of the burning cars, and sought a nail in the rubble. After nearly a decade of war with Iraq, and now harassment by Iranian counterrevolutionaries, even common nails were at a premium.

He found a nail—a thick one with a large square head—amid the ruins of the Museum of Iranian Art and Archaeology. He carried it back to his shop and, using a wooden mallet, drove it into the wall in a new spot.

He was hanging the portrait of the Ayatollah when the Western woman walked in. Masood knew she was a Westerner because, contrary to Islamic law, she wore no face-concealing *chador*. Her skirt hung well below her knees, but shamefully, her ankles and calves were bare. Masood found himself staring. It had been a long

7

time since he had seen a young woman's naked legs. Not since before the Revolution.

To his surprise, the woman inquired of his health in impeccable Farsi.

"*Salaam. Hale shoma chetore?*" she asked.

"*Khube,*" he replied "*Shoma?*"

When the woman replied that she was fine, he stepped down and asked her if she sought a special rug.

The Western woman shook her head, saying "*Na, na.*"

"I have many fine rugs," Masood repeated in the same language.

Her eyes sought the hanging portrait.

"Such a large nail," she ventured, "for such a small portrait."

Masood frowned. "The Imam deserves the best," he said.

"And very old."

"I found it in the rubble of the Archaeology Museum. It is a crime. So many fine artifacts in ruins."

"In the Archaeology Museum, you say?" Her black eyes were thoughtful. "It could be anything then. Even a relic."

"A nail is a nail," Masood Attai said, shrugging expressively.

Reluctantly the woman turned to a fine Ghiordes prayer rug. She knelt, showing the trim line of her thighs. She was a very fine woman. A thoroughbred, Masood thought. She tugged at the corners with expert fingers.

"Have you any Mamluks?" she asked upon returning to her feet.

"Alas, no," Masood said. "Not since the fifth year."

The woman did not ask the fifth year of what. She evidently knew that in modern Iran time was measured since the Revolution.

"I will come again, then," the woman said. And she

clicked out of the shop and into the street without a sign of fear on her comely face.

Another rocket struck moments later. It demolished a green-tiled mosque down Firdausi Street, in the direction the woman had walked. Masood looked out of his shop doorway and saw the woman turn down a side street with quick, businesslike steps. Her chiseled profile was knit in thought. It reflected no other emotion and Masood wondered what it would be like to enjoy such a woman on a cool spring night. . . .

Returning to his shop, Masood noticed that the last concussion had caused the portrait of the Ayatollah to tip. He restored it, wiping ancient dirt off the square nail head with a sleeve. It seemed to be just an old nail. Why had the woman displayed such interest in it? he wondered.

1

Lamar Booe tossed on the narrow cot. He could not sleep. At first it was because the cot, like all the others jammed into the hold, continually shifted and creaked as the great ship plowed through the swells. Then, after the cots stopped shifting, it was because Lamar knew that meant the ship had entered smooth water.

The Reverend-Major came down from the deck to confirm it.

"We're in the Gulf," he whispered, going from cot to cot, shaking the men awake. They reached under their cots for their tunics. They pulled them over their undershirts. Only afterward did they begin assembling their weapons. Bolts slid into receivers. Magazines clicked into ports. Safeties were tested.

The Reverend-Major touched Lamar Booe on the shoulder.

"We're in the Persian Gulf," he whispered.

"Pershing Gulf," Lamar corrected. "When we're done, the world will call it the Pershing Gulf."

"Old Black Jack would be proud." The Reverend-Major smiled. It was a beatific smile. Not the smile of a soldier about to take a force into combat, but of a man of God leading his flock to righteousness. The smile soothed Lamar's anxious soul.

He reached for his staff. Unlike the others, he would not carry a weapon into battle with the heathen. He sat on the side of the cot, the staff across his knees. They trembled a little. He tightened his grip. He had kept the staff on the bed with him throughout the night because he didn't want the greasy floor to get to the standard he was chosen to carry into battle against the forces of darkness.

Lamar had also slept in his white tunic. The gold stitching across the front gleamed faintly in the weak light.

They waited in the darkness. Some prayed quietly, half-audibly. The close air tasted of oil, heavy and moist. It had made some of them ill—so ill they could not eat, and so nauseated from not eating and the constant rolling motion of the ship that many of them suffered from the dry heaves. A few ate just to have the relief of something to vomit up from their stomachs.

The Reverend-Major, trying to keep their minds off the uncertainty of what lay ahead, walked among them, wielding a rodlike aspergillum and sprinkling blessed water on their heads. An M16 rifle hung from his shoulder. His tunic was purple, of fine silk. It was a proud garment, Lamar thought.

It was a proud venture, bold and good in the eyes of the Lord. Then why were his knees trembling? Lamar wondered. From a pocket inside his tunic, he took a miniature Bible and opened it to a random page. He forced his eyes to read. They skimmed the text, but the light was too dim and he could not concentrate, not even on the sweet word of God.

The Reverend-Major began speaking.

"We fear not the missiles of the Iranians," he said.

"Amen," they returned.

"We fear not the wrath of their mulllahs," he intoned. His eyes lifted to the darkened ceiling as if to a blacked-out heaven.

"Amen."

"For we know that God has chosen us to be his instruments."

"Hallelujah!" they chorused, their voices lifting.

"And we will triumph," said the Reverend-Major.

"We know this!"

"I will now bless the weapons of any who wish me to do so," the Reverend-Major said quietly.

The men collected into a ragged line. Lamar had no weapon in need of blessing. Besides, he wasn't sure his legs would be steady enough to carry him. He knew he would be ready when the time came. But not now. Not just now. His hands whitened on the staff that had been sanctified and personally presented to him by God's Right Arm of Earth, the Reverend-General himself.

He knew its holy strength would be his when the time came. For Lamar Booe had faith. And faith was all he would ever need.

But when the muffled toots of the tugboats came through the hull, his hands started to shake.

The great ship was being steered into the loading dock.

Rashid Shiraz smiled when he saw the old tanker, the *Seawise Behemoth*, appear in the Gulf. He picked up his field glasses and watched as the tugboats surrounded it and, like waterbugs pushing the carcass of a beetle, muscled it closer to the Kharg Island oil facility, on the Iranian side of the Persian Gulf.

Another tanker had made it through the perilous Strait of Hormuz. It was the second in two days. That was good, Rashid thought. Iran would need all the foreign currency its oil could generate.

But as Rashid trained his eyes on the wallowing black tanker, a furrow of perplexity appeared between his heavy eyebrows.

There was something odd about the tanker. Something wrong. He raked the stern with his glasses. Seamen busily made ready to lash the tanker to the loading facility. All seemed normal on deck.

Rashid examined the hull through his glasses, although he did not know why. He was a member of the Pasdaran, the Iranian Revolutionary Guard. It was his job to guard Kharg Island from aggression—although he sometimes wondered what the clerics in Tehran expected his unit to do if an enemy rocket came down on Kharg. Or if an American warship heaved to and issued that dreaded warning to abandon the facility.

A vertical line of white numerals showed at the bow of the *Seawise Behemoth*. The furrow between Rashid Shiraz' thick eyebrows became a knife slice.

"This is wrong," he muttered. "This is very wrong."

He hurried to the manager in charge of the facility.

"There is a danger from that tanker."

The manager had been in charge of Kharg Island since the days of the Shah. He was politically suspect, but the Revolution needed his expertise more than it lusted for his blood, so he was allowed to remain on the job.

He looked at Rashid with no fear. Just a veiled contempt.

"What you say?" he demanded.

"Look," Rashid said, handing him the field glasses. "At the bow. See the waterline?"

Reluctantly the man did as he was bidden. He fixed the glasses on the bow of the ship.

"You see it? The numbers?" Rashid demanded. "It is too low to the water."

The manager saw the column of white numerals above the waterline. They were the plimsoll marks, and indicated the tanker's draft in feet. When the tanker was full of oil, only numbers in the high sixties or seventies would show. When it was empty it would ride very high above the water, and it would be possible to see numbers as low as twenty-five. But on this craft the number forty-seven was visible above the Gulf's turquoise waters.

"What could they be carrying?" The manager's voice was puzzled.

"Then I am right! They do not come with empty holds."

"No," the manager said, taking the glasses from his eyes.

"No sane tanker captain would bring oil into the Gulf."

"A leak perhaps," the manager muttered. "They are taking on water."

"They would have sunk with such a leak, am I right? Tell me. Say that I am right."

The manager said nothing. He would not admit that Rashid was right, he hated the man so.

"What can it mean?" the manager asked at last. He might as well have asked the wind, because Rashid was no longer there. He was running down to the docks where the tugs were easing the black monster into position. He was shouting.

"No one comes off that ship! That ship is quarantined! I decree it in the name of the Revolution!"

The *Seawise Behemoth* lay just off the terminal. Within a matter of minutes it was surrounded by the speedy attack boats of the Revolutionary Guard. One boat pulled up to the terminal to pickup Rashid. He ordered it alongside the *Seawise Behemoth*.

An aluminum ladder was lowered from the side of the big oil tanker. Rashid was the first to go up. His AK-47 was slung across his back. He unshipped it the moment his boots touched the deck plates. He pointed it at the captain.

"What means this?" the captain, who was Norwegian, demanded hotly.

"I am Rashid Shiraz, of the Iranian *Pasdaran-e Engelab*. I intend to search your ship for contraband."

"Nonsense. I come for oil."

"You have nothing to fear if you are not engaging in counterrevolutionary activities," Rashid said as his fellow Revolutionary Guards slipped over the deck.

"Two teams," Rashid called. "Hamid, you take one. The others will come with me. Quickly. Search everywhere!"

"For what?" Hamid asked doubtfully.

"For a bad thing," Rashid said, leading his team off.

Hamid's team went in the other direction, not knowing what bad thing Rashid meant, but certain that they would know it when they saw it.

Rashid was tearing the captain's personal quarters to pieces, despite the captain's strenuous protest, when, somewhere deep within the ship, a machine gun burped. It was so brief a sound that Rashid called for his Pasdaran to cease smashing the captain's desk with axes so he could listen for it again.

The next burst was long. There were answering shots. Pistols. Then more automatic-weapons fire.

"Follow me!" Rashid cried, throwing himself up a companionway.

On deck, the sounds were louder. They came from amidships. It was a long run to amidships, for although not a supertanker, the *Seawise Behemoth* was not small. Rashid was out of breath when he came to the companionway from which the sounds of conflict crackled.

A man stumbled up from the hold. His mouth bled. He was Iranian. His stomach suddenly blew out like a bad tire. Viscera splattered Rashid, who recoiled from the spray. Bullets coming through the man's stomach knocked one of his own men down.

Rashid recognized the gut-shot man as belonging to Hamid's team. With hand motions, he signaled his men to stay clear of the opening. They huddled behind bulkheads, under pipes, and around the mouth of the companionway, and they waited.

The gunfire was less frequent now. It snapped and spit. There were screams in Farsi. And in another language, a curious word:

"*Hallelujah!*"

Every time a man screamed, a chorus of voices shouted, "Hallelujah!" What did it mean?

Then there was silence and Rashid waited, wiping sweat off his upper lip, where the hair was sparse and straggly.

A man stepped out of the darkness of the ship. He was unarmed expert for a long pole. He wore a shapeless white garment over ordinary Western trousers. From his vantage point, Rashid caught a glimpse of gold stitching across his chest. He could not make out the design.

But when the man set the pole on the deck and shook it once, sharply, so that a white flag unfurled, Rashid understood as much as he could about this sudden madness.

For in the upper corner of the white flag was a gold cross, and it was the cross, Rashid realized, that was stitched onto the man's chest—the symbol of Christendom.

Rashid moved in. He knocked the man in the temple with the butt of his rifle and dragged him off to one side. He was just in time.

Others, also attired in white tunics emblazoned with the cross, surged out of the hold. But these infidels carried automatic weapons.

Rashid cut the first man down. His fellow Pasdarans joined in. Soon a pile of bodies choked the stairwell.

There were shouts of confusion from below. From men blocked by their own dead.

Rashid pulled the pin on a grenade, and reaching around, tossed it below. A flash of fire made a momentary appearance; then there was smoke and high-pitched screaming.

"You, you, and you," Rashid called, pointing to three of his bravest men. "Go down there."

They ran down the hatch. One was blown back by a wall of concentrated fire. He fell in two sections, an upper half and a lower half.

But the others got through. The sounds of a close-quarters firefight came from below.

"Now, all together, charge them!"

Rashid's men piled down into the hold. The fire was terrific. Rashid hunkered down in case stray bullets punched through the thick deck plating. He squatted on his prisoner. When this was over, Rashid's superiors would demand answers. This unarmed infidel would be the one to provide those answers.

Seven Pasdarans had descended into the bowels of the tanker.

Four returned. They looked at Rashid with surly blood-splattered expressions.

"We are done," one of them said.

"The infidels are all dead?" Rashid asked, coming to his feet.

"See for yourself," he was told.

"Watch this man," Rashid warned. "Do not kill him."

Rashid went below. The passageway was strewn with bodies. Gold crosses were red with fresh blood. One man wore a purple tunic. Rashid turned him over with a boot. Breath hissed through the man's bared teeth. He was still alive. Rashid ended his life with two bullets in the stomach and three more in the face. The man's face broke like a dropped mirror.

Rashid worked his way forward, stepping over hands and bodies. The trail of corpses led into a long room filled with overturned cots. A few bodies lay there, huddled in corners, as if these warriors had shrunk from the conflict and were eradicated where they cowered.

Rashid Shiraz returned to the deck.

"What does this mean?" one of his Pasdarans asked him.

"It means—" Rashid began. He looked down at the unconscious man in the white tunic and began kicking him in the ribs, slowly and methodically. "It means war," he said at last.

2

His name was Remo and he wasn't going to jump. No matter how much the crowd begged him.

It had started with one man. The fat guy in the peach-colored hooded sweatshirt. He had been walking along the street ten stories below on the cracked sidewalk. He looked up. It was as simple as that. The guy just happened to look up.

He saw Remo sitting on the ledge of the dirty brick apartment building, his legs dangling over space.

The guy in the sweatshirt stopped dead in his tracks. He turned his body to get a better look. It was nearly dusk now, the air cool.

"Hey!" the guy had shouted up at Remo.

Remo, who had climbed the plaster-chunk-strewn steps of the apartment building to the roof because he wanted to be alone with his thoughts, at first attempted to ignore the man.

"Hey, you. Up there!" the man repeated.

Remo pointedly stared off toward the Passaic River and the gray spire of Saint Andrews Church. He used to go to Saint Andrews as a boy. Every Sunday at eight in the morning, and none of this modern alternative-service-on-Saturday-afternoon crap either. He had been raised by nuns. They were strict. Especially Sister Mary Margaret, who ran Saint Theresa's Orphanage, where Remo had spent the first sixteen years of his life. He never thought he would feel nostalgic about Saint Andrews or the orphanage. But he did. He wished he could drop in and say hello to Sister Mary Margaret and tell her thanks for being so strict and for showing him the right way. But he couldn't. Saint Theresa's had been razed years ago. He had no idea what had become of Sister Mary Margaret.

Down the street, the peach sweatshirt was determined to be heard.

"Hey, buddy, I'm talking to you—you bastard!"

Reluctantly Remo looked down at the man.

"Go away," he said. His voice was even, quiet. But it carried.

"You gonna jump?" the peach sweatshirt called up.

"No chance," Remo said.

"You sure?"

"Yeah."

"You look like a jumper."

"And you look like the worst judge of character since Neville Chamberlain. Now, beat it."

"I think you're a jumper. You got that look. Kinda sad. I'm staying."

"It's a free country. Despite Neville Chamberlain." Remo stared north. He tried to spot the old Rialto Theater. It used to be on lower Broad Street. There was nothing on Broad Street. Just a row of storefronts that looked like Hiroshima after the bomb fell. He wasn't surprised that the Rialto had been shut down. This part of Newark, New Jersey, had gone to hell a long time before. But it would have been nice to see the old marquee. Remo felt nostalgic about that too.

Down on the sidewalk the peach sweatshirt was talking.

"I think he's gonna jump," he said. Remo looked down. The fat guy was speaking to two teenagers with green hair and black leather clothes.

"Oh, wicked," the pair said in unison.

"Hey, guy," one shouted. "We're here. So what's the holdup?"

"Oh, great," Remo mumbled.

"He said he wasn't going to jump, but look at him

perched up there. What else would he do?" This from peach sweatshirt.

"Probably a druggie," one of the green-haired teenagers was saying. "They're always going into abandoned places and doing weird shit. Hey, man, if you're going to jump, could you do it by seven o'clock? I wanna get home in time for *Wheel of Fortune.*"

"I'm not jumping," Remo repeated in a weary voice.

"Then what are you doing up there?"

Remo didn't answer. He wasn't exactly sure. He wasn't supposed to ever come near Newark again. Someone might recognize him as Remo Williams, a patrolman who once walked these streets to protect its citizenry. The same Remo Williams who made headlines when he was sent to the electric chair for the senseless beating death of a local drug pusher. Remo hadn't committed that crime. He wasn't believed. They pulled the switch, and when Remo regained consciousness, he was told to forget his past existence.

It hadn't been hard at first. What was there to cling to? He was an orphan who pulled a tour of duty in Vietnam, and a conscientious beat cop whose life had ended tragically. No parents. Few friends. There had been a girlfriend. They had been engaged. The ring arrived at his cell one night, without a note, and only then did Remo give up all hope and resign himself to the inevitable.

Now, twenty years later, Remo could barely remember what she looked like.

All his friends had deserted him on Death Row. That had been part of the frame, which was what it was. A man named Harold W. Smith had engineered the whole thing. It was Smith who had warned Remo never to come back to Newark ever again. It was not the whim of a hard-nosed government official, although Smith was all of that. It was a matter of national security. Remo had broken the rule a couple of times before. But national security had not been compromised in either case.

So what? Remo thought. So what if they discover that Remo Williams is still alive? It wouldn't necessarily link him to Smith, head of the supersecret government agency known as CURE, which had been set up to fight crime outside of constitutional restrictions. There would be a lot of ways to explain Remo's continued existence. The world would never have to know that Remo Williams had been trained in the ancient Korean art of Sinanju to be America's secret weapon in the unending war against her enemies. There wasn't a document or file anywhere that linked Remo Williams to the House of Sinanju, the finest assassins in history. There was no record of Remo's long service to America. He had saved the country from certain ruin several times. Saved the world at least twice that he knew of.

And all he wanted, right now, was to put the two parts of his life together.

Staring out at the shattered pieces of his old neighborhood, he could not. It was as if there were two Remo Williamses. One the orphan boy who grew up in an uncertain world, and the other the heir to the five-thousand-year tradition of Sinanju, which served pharaohs and emirs long before there ever was an America, and which now served this newest and greatest power on earth.

Two Remo Williamses. One an ordinary man. The other, one of the most powerful creatures to walk the earth since the age of the tyrannosaur. Two men with the same memories. But still two different men.

Somehow it didn't seem real anymore. It was hard to look back and accept the early past as his own. Had he ever been that young and that confused?

Down in the street, the three gawkers were now seven. The newcomers were calling for Remo to jump.

"C'mon man. Get it done with!" a black man called. "We don't be having all night."

"One last time," Remo called down. "I'm not jumping."

"And I say he is," said peach sweatshirt. "He just needs to get his courage up."

"That right. He don't wanna audience 'cause he afraid he'll wimp out and everybody laugh. "That right, Jim?"

"Anybody know what happened to the old Rialto?" Remo called out.

"Closed now, man. Video."

"Too bad," Remo said. "I saw my first movie there. It was a double feature, *Mr. Roberts* and *Gorgo*. They don't make double features like that anymore."

"That right for damn sure."

"I went with an older kid, Jimmy something," Remo continued vaguely. "We sat in the first row. The orchestra pit was in front of us. I remember it was a scary black hole. I asked Jimmy what it was and he told me that was where the monsters sat. When the film started, my eyes kept switching back and forth between the screen and the pit."

"Sounds like a good reason to jump to me," someone said. And everyone laughed.

"For the last time, I'm not jumping."

"You could change your mind," peach sweatshirt said hopefully.

"If I do change my mind," Remo warned, "I'm going to make a point of landing on top of *you*."

Peach sweatshirt took a quick two steps backward. Everyone stepped back. They moved out onto the street. Cars had to stop for them, and when they did, drivers got out to crane their heads in the direction of peach sweatshirt's excitedly pointing finger.

The word "jumper" raced through the gathering throng.

Remo groaned. If this got on the evening news, Smith would kill him. Why did it always go like this? Why couldn't he just be left alone?

Being alone was what this night was supposed to be about. Remo reached for a loose brick near his hand. He wrenched it out of the crumbling mortar with an easy flick of his wrist. Holding the brick in one hand, he began whittling off sharp slivers with the heel of his other hand. The tiny shards shot off from the brick like angry hornets. One tore through peach sweatshirt's hood. He howled at the annoying sting. A second shard caught him in the knee. Peach sweatshirt fell to the ground clutching his leg.

With a rapid-fire series of strokes, Remo sent more brick shards flying. He made it look easy. For Remo, it was. But only years of training in the art of Sinanju made it possible. Years of training in which he first learned to become one with an inanimate object, so that if he wished the brick to come loose, he knew exactly where to take hold of it, exactly how much pressure to apply, and from what angle. A casual glance at the brick's surface told him the weak points—the places where he would get maximum disintegration with minimum force.

He chopped more shards free. The brick was disappearing in his hand. Down below, the crowd was being peppered by a dry stinging rain. The pedestrians began to retreat. A few broke into a run. Drivers scrambled for their cars and got the engines started even as brick slivers cracked their windshields.

Within a matter of seconds, the street was clear of traffic.

Remo smiled. He still had half the brick left. He replaced it in the cornice and stood up.

He wondered what Sister Mary Margaret would say if she could see him now. No, that was the wrong thought. If she could see him now, all she would see would be a young man of indeterminate age. Dark hair, brown catlike eyes, high cheekbones, and unusually thick wrists. Nothing special, at least on the surface. Remo's clothes—a white T-shirt and tan chinos—would have brought a disapproving tsk-tsk from Sister Mary Margaret.

But surface appearances are deceptive. Remo walked to the chimney. It was in the shadow of this chimney one humid summer night that he sat under the stars drinking a beer from a bottle, watching the heavens, and wondering where he would end up, now that he had been drafted into the Marines. Then the world was about to open up to him. He had no inkling of where it would all lead.

He had wondered what Sister Mary Margaret might have said on that night too. The thought made him feel guilty. But he had a right to the beer because he was of age. Still, he had felt guilty.

It had been a long time since he'd felt guilty about his actions. There were a lot of bodies in their graves because of Remo Williams and the work that he had been trained to do. Criminals, enemies of America, yes. But bodies nevertheless. Sister Mary Margaret would have been horrified. Funny he would think of Sister Mary Margaret again. Probably because Chiun wasn't around. Remo had wanted to get away from Chiun, from Smith, and from Folcroft Sanitarium, where he now lived—if occupying a cubicle in an insane asylum could be called living.

At first, it had been a welcome relief from all the years of hotel rooms and safe houses. But after a year, it had begun to grate on his nerves. It was not real living. And Smith was always around. Chiun was always around too, but then, Chiun had been around for most of Remo's adult life. Like Sister Mary Margaret during his childhood.

And so Remo had come to the brick building where he'd lived in a dingy walk-up apartment after leaving the orphanage. He moved back in after Vietnam, and left it a second time only to go to jail. Now the apartment house was deserted. The apartment itself was inhabited by rats, with drug paraphernalia in the halls and obscene graffiti everywhere.

Once, Remo had dreamed of buying the whole building. But after all these years of unsung service, America couldn't even give him a home to call his own.

Remo had started for the roof trap when he sensed

movement below him. He didn't hear anything. The moving thing was too silent to make a sound. Instead, he felt the eddies of disturbed air on his bare forearms. Remo's instant alertness relaxed slightly.

"Chiun?" He said it aloud. "Little Father, is that you?"

A bald head poked up from the open trap. The parchment face of Chiun, reigning Master of Sinanju, regarded Remo wisely.

"Who else moves like a breathless wind?" Chiun's squeaky voice demanded. A wise smile animated his wispy beard.

"Me."

"No, not like a breathless wind. You move like a breaking wind."

"I'll settle for second best," Remo said amiably.

"Breaking wind is not second best, breaking wind is unpleasant. And smells bad."

"Oh." Remo frowned. "That kind of breaking wind."

"What other kind is there?"

"Never mind," Remo said. He sighed. Chiun was in a snotty mood. He could sense it. That was not so bad. When Chiun displayed his good side, it usually meant that he was trying to con something from Remo. Remo wasn't in the mood for the happy Chiun tonight, but a snotty Chiun, he could take. No Chiun at all would have been better.

"Pull up a brick," Remo suggested.

"I will stand," Chiun said, rising from the trap like a child's balloon. He settled on sandaled feet, his green kimono fluttering with motion. Chiun tucked his long-nailed fingers into the garment's belling sleeves and waited. After nearly a minute of silence he cleared his throat noisily.

"Did I forget something?" Remo asked.

"You forgot to ask me how I knew that you would be here."

"I stopped being surprised by you a long time ago."

"Very well, since you will not ask, I will answer anyway."

And Remo leaned against the chimney and folded his arms. Might as well listen.

"You have been acting strangely all week," Chiun pointed out.

'I've been thinking a lot lately," Remo returned.

"As I said, strangely. For you, to think is strange, possibly weird. This is how I noticed. Then you disappear without telling me."

"Can't I just go for a walk?"

"You took a bus."

"I got tired of walking. So what? And how did you know I took a bus? Smith's computers tell you that?"

"No, I knew you would be going. And Smith's secretary told me you did not have her call for a taxicab. You are too lazy to walk far, therefore you took the bus."

Chiun smiled placidly.

"Okay, I took the bus. Big deal. But I don't believe for a moment you knew I was going to leave. It was a sudden impulse."

"It has been building up inside you for six days, no more, no less."

"Six days?" Remo said vaguely. "Let's see, today is Friday." He began counting backward on his fingers. He went through his left hand, and then ticked off his second thumb and called it Sunday. Remo's frowning expression burst into surprise. "Hey! That's right. I started feeling this way last Sunday."

"Precisely," Chiun said.

"Okay, Sherlock. If you have it down to a science, what's bothering me? I hadn't exactly sorted it out myself."

"It is many things. A yearning for home is paramount. I sensed that from the start. That is why I knew you would come here, to Newark. You have known no other place in your sorry existence."

"It hasn't been so bad."

"Have you visited with Sister Mary Margaret yet?"

"Now, how did you know I was even thinking of her?"

"Before me, you had no one. But Sister Mary Margaret raised you."

"All the nuns raised me."

"But she is the only one you ever speak about."

"Well," Remo said, "I haven't seen her. I don't even know where to find her, or even if she's still alive. The orphanage is long gone."

"Your past is long gone, but I understand your yearnings. Sometimes I miss the village of my youth, the pearl of the Orient called Sinanju."

"How anyone could miss that mud hole is beyond me."

Chiun looked around him disdainfully.

"I could say the same of your sordid environment."

"Touché," Remo said. "But you haven't finished. What am I doing here?"

"You wish a place you can call your own. You thought that place was to be found in your past. But having come here, you now understand that you have outgrown this place."

"Fine. I admit it. Just to avoid prolonging this conversation. There's nothing back here for me. Not even Sister Mary Margaret. Besides, she never visited me once on Death Row."

"And it still hurts."

Remo looked away quickly. "She probably figured I was guilty, like everyone else. Or maybe she didn't know."

"After all these years, it still haunts you. That you might have disappointed her."

"Not me."

"No, not you. Never you. For as long as I've known you, you deny your deepest feelings."

"Something's missing from my life, Chiun. I really feel it now that I've seen Newark again."

"Yes, Remo. Something is missing. And I know what it is."

"What?"

"Me."

"No, I don't mean you."

Chiun's face shrank.

"Don't take it personally," Remo said dryly. "But I did live a few years before Smith put you to training me."

"An unimportant prelude to your existence," Chiun said dismissively. "Banish those years from your mind."

"I feel empty, Chiun."

"You are filled with the sun source. You are the first white man so blessed. Although it was a long struggle, with you fighting me every step along the path, I have made you whole. I have made you Sinanju."

"Empty," Remo repeated. "See that?"

Chiun looked. His clear hazel eyes narrowed questioningly.

"That spire?" he demanded.

"Yeah. I used to go to church there."

"So?"

"I haven't been to church in a long time," Remo said wistfully. "Maybe I should go."

"Why do you not, if it means so much to you?"

"I don't know. I haven't thought about religion in years. I guess I feel self-conscious."

"White as you are, I do not doubt it," Chiun said critically.

"Don't be that way. I meant self-conscious about the things that I do. I was a Catholic, you know. We're supposed to confess our sins to cleanse our souls."

"Ah, I understand now. You are embarrassed to confess your terrible heinous sins."

Remo's face lit up. "Yeah. That's it."

"You think that forgiveness is beyond the priest's province."

"Something like that. You really understand, don't you?"

"Yes. And let me allay your fears. Go to the priest. Confess your transgressions, and if he balks at forgiving you, tell him that the Master of Sinanju has forgiven you for the years of insults and humiliation you have heaped upon his frail shoulders. And if he further hesitates, tell him that if the victim of your many sins is so forgiving, how can a lowly priest be any less generous?" And Chiun smiled.

Remo glowered.

"Those weren't the exact sins I was worried about," he said.

"No?" Chiun's cheeks puffed out in disappointment. "What other sins have you committed, Remo?"

"All this killing."

"Killing? How is ridding the earth of vermin in the service of an emperor sinful? I do not understand."

"In the religion I was raised in, all killing is wrong."

"Nonsense. If that were so, then your priests would have deserted these murderous shores long ago. For if there is any sin in killing, it is the sinfulness of killing without pay, or in passion, or for mere greed."

"All killing," Remo repeated firmly. "I put it out of my mind for a long time, but it's starting to bother me. A lot of things are starting to bother me."

"Then go confess. I will wait here."

"Can't. It won't work."

"Then I will go with you, and if the selfish priest refuses to ease your conscience, then I will eliminate him and we will search until we find a properly righteous and generous priest."

"Doesn't work that way, Little Father. Besides, I can't tell anyone—even a priest—about the work I do. CURE operates outside the Constitution. If it gets out that we've been holding America together illegally, we might as well go back to being a colony of England. No. Smith would have to have the priest killed to preserve the organization's security. Not that I believe it's necessary, but that's what Smith would do."

"So? You would already be forgiven by that time."

"That's not the point. Every mission I undertake after that would only pile more sin on my soul. I can't go to confession every time I come back from a mission, knowing that Smith or you would have to take care of the priest."

"This religion of yours," Chiun said. "It has you completely in its insidious power."

"Not really. I haven't gone to church in a long, long time."

"But after all these years, its grip still clutches your heart."

"I'm troubled. That's all. Never mind. I can sort it out. Why don't you leave me alone for a while? I'll come back to Folcroft when I'm done."

"You cannot."

"Why not?"

"Because Smith has a mission for you."

"I'm not in a mission mood," Remo said sourly.

"It is a minor mission. It will not take long."

"Why don't you go, then?"

"I cannot. I have a minor mission too."

"Two missions?"

"Minor missions," Chiun corrected.

"What are they?"

"Nothing of consequence. A skyjacking for you. Another skyjacking for me."

"Two skyjackings? Coincidence?"

"Perhaps. But Smith has sent me to find you so that we may settle these trivial matters."

"How many people at risk?"

"Hundreds."

"Then I guess my problems can wait," said Remo, heading for the trapdoor.

"If you call such trifles problems," Chiun said, trailing after him. "Now, I have problems. . . ."

When they reached the street, a prowl car was drawing up. Two uniformed police stepped out, and shielding their eyes against streetlamp shine, struggled to see the rooftop.

"Looking for the jumper?" Remo asked casually.

"Yeah, you see him?" the driving cop asked suddenly.

"Sure did. I just talked him down."

"Any description?" the second cop wanted to know while the first one pulled out a pencil and pad of paper.

"Let's see now," Remo said slowly. "I'd say he was about five-foot-five, weight one-eighty, age about twenty-seven, brown on brown, wearing jeans with a hole in the right knee. He had on a hooded peach sweatshirt and orange sneakers. He went up that street just a few minutes ago."

"Thanks," said the first cop as they both piled back into the car.

"If you find him," Remo offered, "I'd stick him in the psycho ward if I were you. He kept ranting about jumping. Over and over. He sounded obsessed with the idea."

"Don't worry. He's as good as caught," said the driving cop. "That was a pretty sharp description, by the way. Ever consider a career in law enforcement?"

"Furthest thing from my mind," Remo said as the car pulled out into the street, dragging loose newspapers after it.

Chiun looked up at Remo's grinning face with undisguised puzzlement.

"You are wearing your mischievous face," he said slowly.

"Not me," Remo said pleasantly. "I'm just trying to prevent a disturbed citizen from going over the edge."

3

The sun had set at Newark airport when Remo stepped out of the cab and paid the driver. Chiun joined him as the cab departed.

"There is your conveyance," Chiun said, gesturing carelessly at an idling Marine helicopter.

"Gotcha," Remo said. "But I don't see yours."

"I do not need a conveyance to achieve my mission," Chiun said loftily.

"No? Have you picked up pointers from watching *Flying Nun* reruns?"

"I do not grasp your meaning, Remo. But I need no vehicle because I have already reached my objective."

Just then, a pair of ambulances roared by, sirens howling. They careened between two terminals and hurtled onto the runway system.

"Wild-guess time," Remo said. "Your skyjacking is here. Blink if I'm warm."

Chiun smiled thinly. "You are very astute."

"So where's my skyjacking?"

"In a different place altogether."

"What place?" Remo asked evenly.

"I do not know. I do not pay attention to trifles concerning missions that are not mine. Perhaps your pilot can tell you. I would ask him. Yes, ask him."

"I'll get you for this," Remo promised, heading for the helicopter. He ducked under the drooping blades and they started picking up speed.

"Let me guess," Remo said to the pilot over the helicopter whine. "Los Angeles?"

"Honolulu."

"That's thousands of miles away!"

"That's why I'm just taking you as far as McGuire. They've got a C-141 StarLifter waiting for you there."

"A StarLifter. That sounds military."

'Military Air Command. They're interservice."

"It's probably too much to hope that the military have installed in-flight movies since I was in the service."

"That's pretty good, pal. I hope you've got a lot more jokes like that. The Air Force flyboys will really appreciate some laughs during the ten-hour flight."

"Ten hours," Remo groaned. "It'll probably be all over by the time I get there. Chiun'll have his end wrapped up inside of five minutes and I'll be blamed for botching my assignment."

"You know, I have no idea what you're talking about," the pilot said.

"That's good," Remo said morosely. "Because I couldn't be responsible for your continued existence if you did."

The C-141 StarLifter was designed for transporting men and matériel. For security reasons, Remo wasn't allowed to sit in the cockpit with the pilots. He had to enter through the massive rear ramp. Inside, it smelled of diesel fuel and grease. There were no seats, unless the one in the tank that was cabled down to the floor rails counted.

Remo crawled into the tank and went to sleep, promising himself that Chiun would rue the day he'd stuck Remo with this one.

Remo was coming out of his third catnap when the drone of the engines changed, indicating the StarLifter was coming in on approach. He got out of the tank. Normally he felt refreshed from sleep, but thanks to Sinanju, he couldn't rest more than five hours at a stretch without feeling that he'd overslept. Three three-hour catnaps were an overload.

The StarLifter shuddered when its massive wheels hit the runway, bounced, and settled again. The plane stopped as soon as it lost airspeed, and the loading ramp dropped hydraulically.

"Must be my cue," Remo said.

It was daylight when he emerged onto the runway. Remo looked around as he rotated his thick wrists eagerly.

Off at the far end of the runway a 747 sat idle. A wheeled gangway ramp was resting near the forward cabin door. A man in khaki clothes crouched on the top step. He wore a red checkered *kaffiyeh* over his face so that only his eyes showed. He carried a Kalashnikov rifle.

He was looking at the StarLifter. As Remo watched, he stuck his head back in and gestured wildly to someone Remo couldn't see.

Remo started walking toward him, slightly relieved that the hijacking hadn't ended, if only so he hadn't traveled the width of America for nothing.

The hijacker noticed Remo when he stepped out from under the StarLifter's wing. He yelled something in a foreign tongue Remo couldn't place. Remo waved at him. It was a polite, friendly wave.

But under his breath Remo muttered, "Start the countdown, friend. Your obit is about to be written."

The hijacker lifted his rifle to his shoulder. He took his time aiming. Both he and Remo knew that at this distance the bullet would fall short. The hijacker was waiting for Remo to come within shooting range.

Remo obliged him.

The gunman fired one shot.

Remo read the bullet coming in. He actually saw it leave the muzzle, and because he was trained to sense the trajectories of bullets in flight—especially when they were aimed at him—he knew without thinking about it that the first round would whistle over his head.

It did exactly that.

The gunman fired again.

This time Remo sidestepped casually. The bullet sounded like a glass rod breaking in two as it split the air near his left ear.

Remo made a show of yawning. The hijacker's eyes got wider. He set his weapon on automatic.

The spray of bullets chewed up the sun-softened tarmac. The bullets made mushy sounds going in. There were no ricochets. And because Remo had run in under the path of the bullets, he was unharmed.

The hijacker saw that the lone American, who wore no uniform although he had come from an Air Force aircraft, was not only unhurt, but had cut the intervening space in half.

He fired again. This time the man in the T-shirt ran toward him in a zigzagging but casual manner. He did not stumble or flinch. And he was coming directly for the open hatch.

Swiftly the hijacker stepped back, kicked the wheeled stairs away, and pulled the exit door closed. He wasn't sure why he did that.

"Jamil, why did you not shoot that one?" asked the leader.

"I do not know, Nassif." Jamil put his back to the door, his rifle across his chest. He wiped his hands on the stock. The stock became very shiny.

"He was unarmed."

"I saw his eyes."

"So?"

"They were dark. And very deep."

"So?"

"And dead. They were a dead man's eyes. They unnerved me."

Nassif called out to his men, dispersed through the 747, "All of you. Look for that man. See where he went!"

From the rear of the plane, beyond rows of passengers who sat with tight, tired faces, their hands tied with plastic loops, another *kaffiyeh*-masked gunman called back, "He disappeared under the wing."

"Look to the other side. When he comes out, fire at him through the windows. *Ya Allah!* Hurry!"

Several of the gunmen surged to the opposite side. They tore screaming passengers from their seats and threw them into the aisles. A few were clubbed into unconsciousness to quiet them. The hijackers pressed their cloth-covered faces to the windows.

"Do you see him?"

Heads shook in the negative.

"He must still be under the plane!" Nassif hissed. "Perhaps he is cowering in fear."

"Not that one," Jamil croaked. "I saw his eyes. They were unafraid."

"What can one unarmed man do under this plane except cower?" snapped Nassif, cuffing Jamil angrily.

There came a series of loud *pops* and the nose of the aircraft sank slowly.

Under the plane, Remo withdrew a steellike finger from the last of the front tires. It hissed and settled. Casually he worked his way back to the wing gears. He popped the right-hand tires with the same finger, and performed the identical operation on those on the left. Then he collapsed the hull wheel assemblies.

The 747 now sat on ruined tires. It wasn't going anywhere. Remo hadn't wanted the craft to take off while he figured out the best way into the aircraft.

Normally he would have simply gone into the hatch, fast and furious, and taken out anyone who got in his way. But a 747 usually carried about five hundred passengers on its two decks. There was no telling how many hijackers there were or how they were deployed. Even Remo couldn't clean them all out without bullets flying and grenades detonating. The kaffiyehs told him he was dealing with Middle Eastern hijackers. The worst kind. They might be prepared to martyr the entire craft to make some obscure political point.

So Remo opted for a careful approach. The popping tires would make them jumpy, but there was no way around that.

Remo crouched down under a hull wheel assembly. Years ago, when skyjackings became a popular expression of political discontent, Dr. Smith had made Remo sit through a droning lecture about the structural plans of modern aircraft. Bored, Remo made paper airplanes with the briefing papers and sailed them so they nicked Smith's earlobes, alternating right, left, right, left. Smith, although his pinched face tightened, kept on reading from his prepared notes and showing slides on a big screen until Remo had run out of paper. The experience had convinced him that his superior was not normal, and the realization soured Remo's mood for a month.

Remo tried to remember that lecture now. Some aircraft, Smith had told him, could be accessed through the wheel wells if a person had the right tools. Was the 747 one of those?

Remo stared up the wheel well. He couldn't tell by looking. But he started yanking bolts and undoing screws anyway. He got a panel half-loose. Then he carefully pried it free so that it made no noise.

A woman's travel case fell down. Remo caught it and set it aside. Good. That meant the luggage compartment was above him.

Remo slithered up the wheel well, shrinking his ribs so that he passed through the tightest spot easily.

He found himself lying on rows of tagged luggage. Above his head, feet moved softly, erratically.

Placing both sets of fingers against the ceiling, Remo waited until his questing hands picked up the pressure of moving feet. When he made contact, he moved with the feet, keeping them just above him. The feet stopped. Remo sensed a casual shifting of one foot to the other. Nervousness. But not panic. Good. That meant a hijacker and not a passenger.

Remo withdrew one hand and went to work on the plate above his head. He sheared the heads of the bolts with the edges of his free hand. With the other, he balanced the plate in place, elbow locked against the weight of the hijacker.

Carefully he tested the plate. When he dropped his hand, it lowered a millimeter. Not enough for the man standing on it to notice, but enough for Remo to know that the only thing keeping the plate in place was his hand.

Remo set himself. He heard no other footsteps. But that didn't mean there weren't other hijackers nearby.

Remo jumped back.

Light spilled into the hold. The plate smashed down. A man in khaki and kaffiyeh tumbled down with it. Remo leapt for the opening. It just happened that Remo's right foot used the man's head for a launch point. His skull shattered under the recoil of Remo's kicking leap.

Remo went straight up. He grabbed the overhead molding and spread his feet so that when he let go, they landed on either side of the missing plate.

"Who the hell are you?" a male passenger gasped.

Remo shushed him. "Part of the replacement crew," he whispered. "The airline's tired of paying this crew's overtime."

"You're kidding," the man said, serious-faced.

"Where's the nearest hijacker?" Remo asked.

"In the john. Back of the plane. I think he has the runs. There's another one in the cockpit."

"Any others?"

"On the upper deck," a woman hissed. "Please be careful. My sister is up there."

"I'll try not to wake her," Remo promised. "Anyone know how many hijackers in all?"

"Six."

"No. Only four."

"I think I counted eight."

"Never mind," Remo said, working his way toward the john. "I'll count them myself."

Remo knocked on the lavatory door.

"What is it?" a voice asked in heavily accented English.

Remo said, "Need to use the john. Could you pick it up in there?"

"Who? Who is that speaking?" the man hissed shrilly.

"Hold it down in there," Remo warned. "Passengers are trying to sleep. Now, are you coming out, or do I come in?"

Remo heard a safety click off and gave the hijacker points for being smart enough not to sit on the john with a primed rifle across his lap.

Remo kicked at the door. It burst inward. The interior of the lavatory was very small. There was no way the door could go in and not catch the man.

Remo put his head in and saw that it had done exactly that.

The door was embedded in the wall behind the toilet. Two legs spilled out from under the door edges. An arm came out around each side. The arms quivered. Remo noticed a lump in the face of the door that roughly corresponded to where the seated man's head should be. He hammered out at the lump with a fist, and the quivering stopped.

On his way out, Remo noticed a wheeled tray of drinks in the rear service area. He got behind it and started pushing it up the aisle.

When he got to the closed door of the cockpit, he stopped and knocked impatiently.

"Refreshments," he called loudly. "Anyone want a drink?"

A long silence came from the cockpit.

Then a man pushed the door open and shoved the muzzle of a Kalashnikov into Remo's stomach. Remo could have avoided the weapon easily. But a rifle pointed at his stomach meant that it was not threatening someone who couldn't defend himself. And Remo could.

"Who are you?"

"Don't you recognize me?" Remo asked of the man.

Jamil started. His eyes froze like those of a beached fish.

"Impossible," he croaked.

"Nah, just extra-extra clever."

"What do you want?"

"You gonna surrender or what?"

"Or what?"

"That's what I said. Or what?"

"I do not understand."

"And I don't have time to teach you English. Now, what will it be—coffee, tea, or surrender?"

"I will martyr myself before I surrender."

"Fine. Go martyr yourself. Then see if anyone cares."

"I would rather martyr you," said Jamil, who then pressed the trigger on his Kalashnikov, confident that at point-blank range there was no way he could miss the thin man with the dead, dead eyes.

The Kalashnikov did not give out its customary staccato stutter. It sort of went *bloosh!* The relaxed face of the unarmed American did not change. Jamil frowned. He did not understand. Why didn't the man fall down? He felt a sudden tingling in his hands. And then the tingle turned to a dull pain, and almost as soon as it registered on his brain that his hands were in pain, they seemed to be on fire.

Jamil screamed. He saw that his hands were covered with blood. The whites of his finger bones poked out from the redness of raw exposed flesh. The breech of the rifle was smoking and in ruins.

Then he saw that the muzzle of the Kalashnikov was somehow blocked. It had been crimped, as if by a vise.

And just before his eyes rolled up into his head and Jamil lost consciousness, he saw that the white American was rubbing his fingers on the trailing part of Jamil's own *kaffiyeh* as if to wipe gun grease off them.

Remo stepped over the body.

"You two all right?" he asked the pilot and copilot.

"Yes. Who are you?"

"Next question. And you guys have lost your turn. How many hijackers? I got three."

"Two more."

"They must be upstairs."

"Then we'd better evacuate the plane."

"Too risky," Remo said. "They might start shooting from the windows. Sit tight and I'll take care of them."

"Are you crazy? These people are madmen. You know what they want? They want Reverend Eldon Sluggard brought here for some kind of guerrilla trial."

"Who's Reverend Eldon Sluggard?"

"That's what we asked. They said he was the devil who declared war on Islam. They're on some kind of religious kick. Said they've declared war on Christianity."

"I hope the pope is in his summer place," Remo said. "And what I said before still goes. Sit tight. I'll handle this."

And to make sure, Remo smeared the door latch into cold solder after he closed the cockpit door.

Remo went up one of the plush stairways. He heard the tense breathing half-way up. Two sets of lungs trying to push air through cloth-covered open mouths. They sounded like they were on either side of the stairs. Probably planning to ambush him. Remo shrugged and kept coming.

When he reached the top, one stuck a pistol to his

head, and the other, standing on the other side, prodded him in the ribs with a Kalashnikov rifle.

"Uh-oh," Remo said in mock concern. "Looks like you got me."

"Yes, we do have you. Do not move, please."

"I'm not the one who needs to move. It's you two who can't keep standing like that."

"We can do whatever we wish. We have weapons. We have upper hand, you see."

"And if I move, you'll shoot. Am I right?"

"Of course. Why should we not shoot you?"

"Well, because you're holding an AK-47 and your friend's got a Makarov."

"You know weapons. So?"

"So this. If the Makarov goes off, the bullet will go right through my skull, out the other side, and into your head."

The man in the line of the Makarov's fire blinked.

"On the other hand," Remo added, "if you start with that Kalashnikov, your pistol-packing friend buys it."

"Then one of us will move," the rifleman said.

"But you can't do that either," Remo pointed out.

"Why not?" The Makarov wielder looked worried when he asked the question.

"Because then I'll make my move. I'll take out the guy who's threatening me and then I'll get the one still standing."

"No one moves that fast."

"No?" asked Remo. "Look at your pistol."

"What of it?"

"I got your bullets." And Remo raised his hand, showing a magazine clip. For effect, he thumbed the rounds out one by one. They hit the carpet with soft noises like marbles falling.

Eyes stricken, the Makarov wielder turned his pistol sideways so that the grip turned up to the light. He saw the gaping square hole where the magazine should have been. He swore under his breath.

"Do not worry, my brother," the other one said confidently. "You still have a round in the chamber. And I have a full clip."

Remo shook his head.

"Uh-uh," he said, displaying another clip. This one he squeezed into groaning metal.

The man with the AK-47 steadied his muzzle against Remo's ribs and felt for his magazine with his free hand. Remo knew exactly when he encountered an empty port because the man's flesh turned a little green around the eyes.

"I still have a round in my chamber," he said gratingly.

"True," Remo said. "That means you each have one shot. But only one shot. And I suggest you use 'em fast, 'cause when I count to three, I'm making my move. And we all know how fast I am, right?" And to make his point, Remo gave the Kalashnikov clip another hard squeeze. It creaked like an old door.

"One—" Remo began.

The two gunmen stared at one another in growing panic.

"Two—"

"Shoot him! *Shoot him!*"

"Three!" Remo yelled.

Both weapons erupted. The two shots merged into one single detonation. The man holding the Kalashikov suddenly came down with what the medical examiner would later call "a total disintegration of the facial mask." The pistol man took a round in the stomach that cracked his spine just above the coccyx.

Remo straightened his knees just as the bodies fell to the carpet, turning the blue-and red nap a uniform crimson color.

"It's all in the wrists," Remo said cockily.

He went up and down the aisles, looking for more terrorists. When he found none, he ran back down the stairs and slipped through the open plate and down the wheel well. Before heading off for the StarLifter, he replaced the woman's travel case he had put aside earlier.

As he walked back to the waiting plane, he felt better. The assignment had gone off perfectly. No passengers had died and no hijackers had survived. A clean operation. Smith would be pleased.

Remo wondered how Chiun was doing with his mission. He was worried in spite of his annoyance at Chiun. Skyjackings were tricky. He hoped the Master of Sinanju could handle the situation.

4

The Master of Sinanju regarded the 727 with suspicious hazel eyes. He did not like airplanes. He did not like to fly. Flying was unnatural, although he had to admit sometimes convenient. It was one of the reasons he had taken the problem at Newark airport. The second reason was to give Remo something to think about other than his imagined problems.

Chiun saw that there were five entrances to the captured plane. Any of them would be useful. But one in particular would be best. It was the one in the rear, at the tail.

Chiun floated some distance down the runway, his arms in his kimono sleeves, his head bowed in thought. He was thinking of Remo's words. Remo was concerned about his old religious training. He had wondered if such a day would ever come. The Remo he had first met at Folcroft Sanitarium was a bitter and disillusioned man, betrayed by his country, shunned by his friends. Thoughts of his childhood religion were far from his troubled mind. But Chiun knew that no one who learns a thing as a child ever fully unlearns it. And now Remo's old beliefs had resurfaced. This would have to be dealt with. After the present problem.

When Chiun had walked past the tail, he turned around and began retracing his steps. This time he walked toward the tail, directly in line with the stabilizer and fins.

It was the one blind spot on an aircraft, he knew.

..... were windows on the sides and windows in the nose. But the tail was as open to attack as that of a sleeping dog.

Chiun paced up under the fins and stopped under the hatch. It was closed. There were no stairs.

The Master of Sinanju considered the problem at length. The underside of the craft was well over his aged head. He did not wish to demean himself by leaping for the sealed hatch and clawing his way in. He might rip his kimono. There had to be a more dignified way for a man of his august years to gain entrance to a mere winged conveyance.

Chiun decided swiftly. He reached up and tapped the plane's skin with his long-nailed fingers, testing its strength. Then, with a sound like several soda cans being punctured at once, Chiun's nails disappeared into the hull. He pulled sharply.

The nose went into the air. The tail assembly smacked the runway. It crumpled slightly, but the hatch was now very close to the ground. Chiun had already withdrawn his nails.

The master of Sinanju then slipped his fingers into the tight, rubber-sealed hatch edges. When his hands came away, the door sailed over his head and bounced along the runway like a pinwheel.

Chiun appeared in the rear of the craft like an apparition from another dimension.

The entire complement of passengers, crew, and kaffiyeh-masked gunmen turned and stared at him with openmouthed wonder. They clung to bulkheads and seat backs. The aisle between the seats was a ramp on which standing was impossible.

The Master of Sinanju stamped one sandaled foot sharply. The aircraft shuddered, then with agonizing slowness began to right itself. The front wheels hit the ground with a loud bang.

"Remain in your seats," Chiun said loudly. "I am commandeering this conveyance in the name of the People's Autocracy of Sinanju."

"Sinanju?" It was one of the gunmen. "I have never heard of it."

"That is because Sinanju is in North Korea, where such as you are not welcome."

"You cannot hijack this aircraft."

"Give me a reason why not," Chiun said querulously.

"Because we have hijacked it before you."

"You may have been first, but I have seniority."

The terrorists exchanged masked glances.

"We do not understand."

"Seniority. It is an American concept, which I have decided to adopt. I am the oldest among us. Therefore I am senior. Therefore I have seniority."

"We are in solidarity with People's Democratic Republic of North Korea," one of the gunmen said slowly. "Perhaps we can work together. What is your political objective?"

"To serve my emperor," said the Master of Sinanju as he approached the man. The gunman lowered his rifle. He saw that the Korean was very, very old. The wrinkles in his parchment face were like those of the mummies at the Cairo museum. He looked like no threat. And yet . . .

"I did not know, *mumia,* that North Korea had an emperor," the leader of the hijackers said slowly.

"It does not. I serve the American emperor. Smith."

"What foolishness do you speak?" the leader said hotly. "There is no American emperor called Smith."

"No? Then why does he send me here to bargain with you?"

"Bargain?"

"State your terms," Chiun ordered.

"We have already issued them. We demand that Reverend Eldon Sluggard be brought here for a People's Tribunal."

"Who is this Reverend Eldon Sluggard?"

"He is a Satan of Satans. The devil incarnate on earth. He has declared war upon the Moslem world and in response Islam has declared holy war on him."

"I have never heard of him."

"If this Sluggard is not brought before us, we will martyr all these people," said the leader, sweeping the confines of the aircraft with his rifle barrel.

Passengers cringed. A woman screamed. Another broke down, her shoulders quaking in muffled sobs.

"Have a care where you point that boom stick, Moslem," Chiun admonished. "These people are my prisoners, not yours."

"No. You are our prisoner. We no longer recognize solidarity with your cause. You have admitted that you work for America. Sit down."

"Make me."

"We will kill you dead."

"Is there another result of killing?" Chiun asked in a puzzled voice.

"Bring dead American," the leader called.

As Chiun's face tightened, the two other terrorists went forward and dragged a body back from the first-class compartment.

"See? See what we are capable of?" the terrorist leader said proudly.

The Master of Sinanju padded on sandaled feet to the body. He studied the face, whose open sightless eyes stared at the ceiling. The chin had never known a razor. The boy wore a uniform of some sort.

Chiun turned to the leader of the hijackers. His voice was low when he spoke.

"This one was a mere boy."

"He wore uniform of United States. We spit upon him and all who work with him."

And the terrorist spat on the boy's blood-dappled uniform.

"I have no love for soldiers," Chiun intoned.

"We are soldiers."

"And I have less love for you."

"We do not need your love, *mumia*. We want only your obedience. If you work for America as you say, you will make a fine hostage."

"And you will make an excellent corpse," said the aged Korean. And before anyone could react, the Master of Sinanju had moved on the leader of the hijackers.

Chiun came in low, his body bent at the waist. He made a crouching half-turn. Then he whirled like a top. His feet, lashing out, broke the leader's kneecaps with shattering finality. The man crumpled. The side of Chiun's hand broke his neck before his face struck the floor.

That left two remaining hijackers.

"I will give you your lives if you surrender now," Chiun said. He said this not because he wished to avoid killing them but because he did not want any of the other passengers to be hurt.

The two gunmen, stationed on either side of the door leading to the service area, trained their rifles on Chiun's resolute face. No one moved.

Then Chiun's nose crinkled.

"You!" Chiun lashed out with an accusing finger. "I detect the smoke of death from your weapon."

Something in the voice of the Master of Sinanju caused the accused murderer to hesitate.

"You are the killer of this boy," Chiun accused.

"What . . . what of it?"

"My offer is hereby rescinded. I will not spare you. You do not deserve to live. But you, other man, I may see fit to spare your life if you do exactly as I say."

"What?"

"Eliminate your comrade for me so that I do not have to sully my hands with so odious a task."

"Khalid is my friend. I would not do that."

Chiun reached down and in a deceptively casual gesture flipped the leader's fallen Kalashnikov into his hands. His face wrinkled distastefully.

Then, savagely, methodically, he dismantled the weapon. Steel shrieked. Sparks flew. Wood splintered. Machined pieces were ground to grit between his fingers.

"If I can do this to metal and wood, imagine what I

can do to flesh and bone," Chiun said coolly. He tucked his fingers in his kimono sleeves, and catching the gunman's eyes, shifted his gaze from him to the other gunman.

The gunman understood the signal. He was being given his last chance.

He hesitated. Then, crying, "I am sorry, Khalid!" he sprayed his comrade with a short burst. The other man went down, a bloody and broken rag doll.

Shaking, tears squeezing out of his eyes, the first gunman lowered his smoking weapon to the carpet. He raised his hands in helpless resignation as the tiny Oriental advanced on him, a wise, knowing expression on his countenance.

"You promised me my life," the terrorist sobbed.

Chiun removed his hands from his sleeves and brought them up to the man's pain-racked face.

"I had my fingers crossed," said the Master of Sinanju. And then, untwining his fingers, he punctured the pulsing artery in the man's neck.

While the last gunman lay on the carpet spurting like a squirtgun whose reservoir was near exhaustion, the Master of Sinanju turned to the horrified faces of the passengers.

Lifting his hands, he announced, "These are your tax dollars at work. Remember that the next time you consider cheating your righteous government. For many starving Korean babies will have full bellies because of you. I have spoken."

And bowing once, the Master of Sinanju disappeared from the aircraft and into the night.

5

Remo Williams sensed the change in engine pitch before the StarLifter's multiple turbines climbed into a higher key. The big transport was about to land. Finally. Remo had grown so impatient with the return flight that, because he couldn't force his body to sleep anymore, and because he was bored, he whiled away the hours taking apart the tank cabled to the floor. That had taken half the flight.

Now, as the StarLifter jolted to a landing, Remo was trying to refit the cannon into the big angular turret. He wasn't sure which end was which, but looking at the rest of the tank, with its heavy treads wrapped around its gears like loose rubber bands, and the pile of pieces off to one side that he couldn't remember taking out in the first place, he figured it didn't matter.

And with all the talk about amphibious tanks that sink in three feet of water, it probably wouldn't matter that the Pentagon was short one Bradley Fighting Vehicle.

Remo emerged from the rear of the StarLifter, once again in the middle of a deserted runway.

"Nothing like being the hometown hero," he mumbled. Then he noticed that he wasn't in Newark. The airport looked familiar, but then all airports looked alike to him.

Remo had started walking to the nearest terminal when he saw a familiar face standing in front of a baggage tractor. It was Chiun. As soon as Remo lifted his hand to wave, the Master of Sinanju pretended to become interested in a passing swallow.

"Great. Who's supposed to be mad at whom now?" Remo said aloud.

He walked up to Chiun, making sure every step was audible.

"Remember me?" Remo asked politely. "Your adopted scapegoat?"

"And you smell like one," said Chiun petulantly. "What have you been doing—playing in the mud?"

"Grease," said Remo, showing his black-streaked hands. "I guess I need a change of clothes."

"You will not have time. Already, because of you, I have been forced to wait here for many hours. All through the long night and day. And now, as I watched the sun set for a second time, you finally return, noisy and smelly and late."

"Hey, who stuck who with a twenty-hour round-trip flight to Honolulu?"

"At least you had something to do, you . . . you mechanic," Chiun sputtered.

"All right, all right," Remo said, raising his hands in angry resignation. "Just answer me this. Where are we?"

"Dullsville."

"I thought we agreed to move on to more fruitful areas of discussion."

"I have told you. We are at Dullsville Airport. It is near one of your Washingtons."

"Dullsville . . . Washington," Remo mused. He snapped his fingers. "Right. Washington, D.C. This must be Dulles Airport."

"Dulles, Dullsville—all American places sound alike to these aged ears. As for what we are doing here, Emperor Smith refused to tell me. He said it was for your hearing only, and I am insulted."

"Why?" asked Remo, hurrying into the terminal. Chiun

flew at his heels, skirts blowing with the fury of his pace.

"Because I am still senior Master."

"Smith probably figures he'll save time by explaining it to me and having me explain it to you later. He's always complaining that you're hard to deal with."

"I?" squeaked Chiun, stopping in the middle of the crowd. "I, hard to deal with? Emperor Smith said that? Of me? Poor Chiun? Aged Chiun? Chiun, who is in the end days of his life? Hard to deal with?"

"Excuse me, sir," a skycap who was loaded down with two suitcases under each arm interrupted politely. "You're blocking the way."

Chiun whirled on him with the blunt fury of a tornado.

"You would not have to take up so much room if you did not carry so many suitcases," the Master of Sinanju said scornfully. "Have you never heard of packing light?"

"But these aren't mine," the skycap protested.

"Here, since you insist upon intruding on the serene placidity of my existence, I will relieve you of your burdensome baggage."

And, moving with controlled rage, the Master of Sinanju slashed the handles of the suitcases so that they fell from the skycap's clenching fingers. The luggage, seeming to weigh no more than down pillows, floated to the tips of Chiun's long-nailed fingers and, spinning briefly like gyroscopes, suddenly careened toward an escalator. They landed in a pile. The heaviest pieces, flying open, spilled a profusion of brightly colored garments.

A matronly woman who had been walking behind the skycap screamed in horror.

"My luggage!" she wailed.

All eyes turned to them as the skycap pointed an accusing finger at Chiun.

Remo moved in swiftly, and taking Chiun by the elbow, guided him to an empty phone booth.

"Serene placidity?" Remo asked pointedly as he slid a quarter into the slot.

"That man was rude," Chiun fumed. "I am amazed that he stayed married to that woman for so long."

"I don't think they were married, Little Father. And what was that crap you were giving him about too much luggage—you who won't go on a pleasure-boat ride without taking along fourteen steamer trunks?"

"Which are forever being misplaced by incompetents or having to be shipped separately. And do you know why?"

"Let me guess," Remo said as he dialed the special code. "Because guys like him hog the room that rightfully belongs to *your* luggage."

"That is correct, Remo," Chiun said in a mollified voice. "I am glad you understand."

"No, I don't understand," Remo returned as he listened to the dial-a-joke. When the punch line was about to come in, he inserted his own. "I don't know who he was, but his driver was Gorbachev," Remo recited wearily. He hated Smith's security rigmarole. Then, while a series of phone relays clicked, he returned to Chiun. "He's entitled to his four pieces just as much as you are to your fourteen."

"Philistine," spat Chiun, turning his back.

"Hello, Smitty," Remo said when the parched voice of his superior, Dr. Harold W. Smith, came over the line. "I'm at Dulles. I guess you know that, because you rerouted my flight. What's up?"

"Remo, I don't have much time," Smith said. "I'm on my way to Washington myself."

"Want us to wait for you?"

"No, you and Chiun have a critical task before you. A terrorist group has taken control of the Lincoln Memorial. They have explosives. Fortunately, there are no innocent people involved. The National Guard has the monument surrounded, but one of the terrorists claims he's holding a pressure-sensitive trigger device. If he lets go of it, either voluntarily or in death, the memorial will go up."

"Terrorists? I just dealt with a terrorist hijacking. So did Chiun."

"It's like a plague. The police killed one Middle Easterner while he was attempting to wire Mount Rushmore with explosive charges. Another group simply opened fire in a crowd watching an air show in Dayton, Ohio. It was a slaughter. One perpetrator was captured alive. He's been sent to FBI national headquarters in Washington for interrogation. That's where I'm going. Every few hours, another incident is uncovered. It's as if the terrorist world has declared all-out war on the U.S."

"What else is new?"

"Believe it or not, Remo, as vicious as these people can be, they are very canny and politically astute. Until now they have carefully targeted U.S. interests abroad, but this time there seem to be no restrictions. We have no idea what has triggered this, but it's big. Huge. That's why I'm on my way to Washington. I'm going to personally interrogate this man. The sooner we have answers, the quicker we can move effectively against the instigators. Right now, we're reduced to putting out brushfires."

"Why not let Chiun and me handle the interrogation? We can squeeze the truth out of him faster than you can call your travel agent."

"No good. The Lincoln Memorial is a national symbol. If it goes, even without loss of life, it would be a blow to our national prestige worse than Pearl Harbor. It would show the world that we cannot even protect our nation's capital."

"I guess I follow, but Chiun could have handled this."

"I could not take that chance. I wasn't certain he would understand the technical problem of the detonator."

"I heard that," said Chiun loudly.

"What was that?" Smith asked.

'Chiun. He's pissed. I let slip that you sometimes find him difficult."

Smith sighed. "His feelings will have to take a back seat to this situation."

"I heard that too," Chiun shouted.

"Never mind," Remo put in. "We're off to the Lincoln Memorial."

"Don't let it be destroyed, Remo," Smith warned.

"Not me. Count on it."

Remo hung up and turned to the Master of Sinanju, who fumed, his foot tapping impatiently.

"After all these years," said Chiun. "After all these years of faithful service, now I know how that man truly feels about me."

"Can it, Chiun. Smith has a lot on his mind. Let's grab a cab."

"And who is he to order us around like chess pieces? Without proper rest or nourishment. For too long we have done his bidding. And for what? What?" demanded the Master of Sinanju as he followed Remo out of the terminal and to a taxi stand.

"For gold," Remo said, flagging a cab. He opened the door for Chiun and slid in after him. The cab got going.

"Yes," said Chiun. "For mere gold."

"Gold? Mere? I never thought I'd hear you say those two words together."

"There are more things in life than gold," said the Master of Sinanju.

"I know that, but I didn't know that you knew that. While we're in traffic, regale me with a few choice examples."

"There are coffee breaks. When has Smith ever given us a morning coffee break? Even lowly cabdrivers get those."

The driver peered into the rearview mirror sourly.

"We don't drink coffee, Little Father. Caffeine is like rat poison to our digestive systems."

"It is not the coffee. It is the break. We could have a rice break."

"I'd like a break from eating rice."

"And what about a pension plan? And health insurance?"

"We're assassins. If we live to see our old age, it will be a miracle."

"You perhaps, but I expect to see my old age. Someday. Years from now."

"Uh-huh," Remo said. "I think you're just cruising for a grudge. You can't blame Smith for finding you tough to take sometimes."

"Why? Why? Tell me what I ever did to annoy him."

"For one thing, you carp a lot."

"Carp? Carp? Me? Carp? I never carp. Or complain. Although I have a good reason, what with a white for a pupil and another white for an emperor. And Smith is not even a proper emperor. When was the last time he wore a crown upon his head?"

"Got me. I can't remember the first time."

"I must write these things down. They will all go into my next contract negotiation. In the future I will require that Smith wear a crown when he deals with me. It is what my ancestors were accustomed to. It is what I am entitled to."

"And that's another thing. Your escalating demands. Another five years of contracts, and America will be bankrupt."

Chiun raised a finger. "But safe. And safety has no price. Let the American people work harder. Let them pay more taxes. Do you know that if fewer Americans cheated on their taxes, Smith could afford to pay us more?"

"We should stop in at the IRS when this is over," Remo sighed, folding his arms. "I'm sure they'd be captivated by your collection ideas."

"They are not for sale," Chiun sniffed.

"They pay a finder's fee, you know. Based on percentage."

"When you pay the driver, ask him for the IRA's address."

"That's IRS. The IRA is a different terrorist group. But you could probably find work with them too, if you're so unhappy with Smith."

The driver turned back to face them. They were on the Virginia side of the Arlington Memorial Bridge, which spanned the Potomac River. "This is as far as I can take you two," he said. "Looks like they have the bridge shut down. Must be an accident or something."

"I heard the Lincoln Memorial is under siege," Remo said.

"No shit. Those Democrats sure took the last election hard," the cabby remarked.

"Guess so," Remo said, paying the man off. Chiun followed him through the lines of stalled cars, which honked and grumbled up to the banks of the Potomac.

"This is going to be a tough one," Remo said as the brilliantly lighted Lincoln Memorial came into view. The night was alive with the red and blue lights of official vehicles. There were National Guard troops deployed even on this side of the Potomac.

"Not with me to help you avoid mistakes."

"Smith told me we don't have any innocent lives at stake. So our objective will be to take out the terrorists before they blow up the building."

"I understand."

Remo whirled. "You do?"

"Yes, of course. That fine building is obviously a temple of worship. Is it one of your churches, Remo?"

"No, but it's important. We can't let it go up in smoke."

"I suggest the Flying Dragon attack," Chiun said, surveying the building.

Remo shook his head. "Too wild. We gotta pinpoint

the man with the explosive detonator. Once we take him out, the rest will be just mopping up."

"I do no mopping, up or down," snapped Chiun. "I am no menial. I will consider mopping up when I receive a proper rice break."

"Look, this is very serious. And mopping up is just an expression."

"So is respect. And I see none of it from either Smith or you."

"Simmer down," Remo said, slipping around the ring of National Guardsmen. "The reason Smith didn't brief you on the mission was that he wasn't sure you'd understand about the detonator. It's very tricky stuff."

"What is so tricky about something that goes boom?"

"Not being on the premises when it does go boom," Remo said dryly. "Ask any bomb-disposal expert."

"I will leave boom disposal to you. I will handle the garbage disposal, heh, heh."

"I think our best bet would be to sneak up on the building," Remo said as he studied the Lincoln Memorial, just across the river. It was as still as a photograph. "The National Guard has a clear view of the whole grounds. The terrorists have the same advantage. We should swim for it, then sneak up on the building."

"Ah, the Sea Dragon attack. A sound approach," said Chiun, girding his waist as he headed for the sparkling waters of the Potomac. "Then we will descend upon these villains, faster than a serpent's fangs, and steal the very breath from their mouths."

"Not so fast," Remo said, touching Chiun on the shoulder. "It's more complicated than that."

Chiun turned and looked up at Remo curiously. "How so?"

"I thought you heard what Smith said. About the detonator."

"I only listened to the meaningful portions. The painful words. The low, base lack of appreciation. Besides, we are faster than any finger on any button."

"It's not striking before they push the button this time out, Little Father. We've got to hit them so they don't let go of the button. One of those guys is holding a device. I'm not sure what it looks like. But the instant he lets go, ka-boom!"

Chiun considered. "I liked the old buttons better."

"That's progress. Got any ideas on how to handle this? An appropriate legend about the days of the pharaohs perhaps?"

Chiun frowned. "Pharaohs did not have explosions."

"Let's hope we don't either," Remo said. "And I take it I'm on my own figuring this one out."

Chiun shrugged. "You are an American. You are used to dealing with the irrational."

Remo looked at Chiun and started to say something. He changed his mind and instead said, "No comment. Just follow me. Maybe when we spot the guy with the detonator, something will come to us."

And Remo, moving low to the ground, slipped into the water like a duck, the Master of Sinanju following him. Their heads vanished under the surface so cleanly that within seconds there was no ripple to betray their penetration.

As the cold current of the Potomac closed over them, Remo and Chiun moved through the water like two purposeful dolphins. They held air in their lungs so that no water bubbles betrayed their passing. They were like human submarines, silent, efficient, undetectable. Their lungs contained just enough air to keep them floating under the surface, but not so little that they touched the silty river bottom. Their feet kicked in small controlled motions, their arms trailed at their sides, hands moving like little rudders.

Emerging on the other side of the river, they lurked in the shrubbery while they scanned the situation.

The Lincoln Memorial shone in the glow of its ground spotlights. The long Reflecting Pool it faced was tranquil. The air was cool, but Remo sensed the tension that gripped the night.

"I see no persons," Chiun whispered.

Remo shifted to another vantage point, confident that even the National Guard could not see him. He spotted a figure in khaki. His head was swathed in a black *kaffiyeh*.

"See the one pacing behind the columns?" Remo whispered.

The Master of Sinanju nodded. "He carries a boom stick, but no other weapon."

"He's yours if we have to move quickly."

"He is already history," said Chiun, repeating a phrase he had picked up from American TV.

"Just so the Lincoln Memorial isn't."

Several minutes passed without another person showing himself.

"Guess we might as well get this over with," Remo breathed. "Remember what I said about the detonator."

When he got no answer, Remo looked at the next bush. Chiun was not in sight. Then he saw the Master of Sinanju slip around the side of the Lincoln Memorial.

"Oh, Christ! Chiun! What are you trying to do to me?"

And Remo glided toward the huge illuminated stairs of the Lincoln Memorial. He threw himself up against one of the huge Doric columns. He listened. He heard breathing. Low, tense. The breathing of nervous men. Three of them. He waited. Where the hell was Chiun?

Then suddenly there were only two men breathing.

What the hell? Remo thought.

Then only one man's breathing could be heard.

"Damn!" Remo cursed. He had no choice now. He moved in.

A man slouched in the lee of the entrance to the sanctuary housing the great seated figure of Abraham Lincoln, his AK-47 held in both hands. The figure looked relaxed, the gun muzzle pointing to the limestone flooring.

Remo, sensing no breathing, walked up to the man. His eyelids were lowered, but not closed. He seemed to be looking down the muzzle of his weapon. But when Remo placed a palm under his nose, he felt no exhalation.

The man was dead. Chiun's handiwork. But what was he trying to do? Prove himself to Smith? Remo moved on. The sanctuary looked empty. He made for the statue anyway.

Easing around behind the Lincoln statue, Remo sensed rather than heard a presence. It was close. It was not behind the statue. Nor was it outside.

A pebble struck him on the head and Remo jumped like a cat.

"Shhhh!" a voice hissed. Remo looked up. The Master of Sinanju was perched on Lincoln's shoulder.

"What are you—!"

Chiun laid a finger before his lips. He leapt, floating to the ground like a colorful human parachute.

"I have immobilized two of them. What have you accomplished?" Chiun asked smugly.

"I just got here."

"No rice break for you."

"Shove it. Where's the guy with the detonator?"

A hissing voice answered for him.

"Walid! Mehdi! Where are you?"

"Back that way," Remo whispered, gesturing. "He's our man. This time, no freaking grandstanding, okay?"

"I leave him to you."

"And what are you going to do?"

"Watch. If you are successful, the House of Sinanju will have learned something."

And if I'm not?"

"This," whispered Chiun, lifting closed fists to Remo's face. Remo looked at them closely, his face uncertain.

Chiun suddenly opened his fingers. "Ka-boom," he said. "Heh, heh, ka-boom."

Remo's face snapped back, scowling. "I knew that already."

"Then why did you ask?"

"Because I—" A voice diverted Remo's attention. It was the remaining terrorist. "Better get to cover," Remo said over his shoulder. When there was no answer, he looked back. Chiun had vanished again.

"Thanks a lot for helping me in my hour of need, Chiun," Remo muttered.

A whispered "You are welcome" reached his ears. It was so soft that it sounded inside his head, like telepathy.

Remo decided he needed a vantage point. He went up Lincoln's back like a spider. He rested, his arm around the Great Emancipator's cool white marble neck. He spotted the second terrorist, stiff as a plank on the floor. Chiun had obviously come up from behind him, applied a Sinanju death grip, and carefully lowered him to the ground. The Master of Sinanju hadn't taken any chances that either man had the detonator. He had used a paralyzing death grip that accelerated the rigor-mortis process.

"Walid!" It was the third terrorist. "*Biya enja!* Come here!" His voice had risen two octaves. He was very nervous. Remo zeroed in on him. He crouched in one of the side rooms, beyond the dividing wall of Ionic columns. He had no rifle. But his hands squeezed a black object that looked a little like a flashlight. From the bottom, wires trailed off in three directions. Remo followed one of the wires with his eyes. It led to a satchel charge of some kind strapped around the man's waist. The other wires probably went to two strategic locations.

There was no approach to the terrorist other than a direct one. Remo took it. He scrambled down off the statue, landing at Lincoln's feet. Then, casually, his hands hanging loosely at his sides to show that he was unarmed, Remo stepped into the next chamber, where the Gettysburg Address was carved into a wall.

"Hi, there!" Remo called. He smiled. He gave it his disarming best. There would be no room for mistakes now.

"Stay back, you . . . you American. You Satan!" the terrorist warned. He clutched the device in his hands more tightly, all but concealing it in his big fists. His thumbs were linked over the device's top. Probably where the button was, Remo decided.

"Satan? Me? You're the guy who's threatening U.S. government property. Don't you know there are laws against this kind of stuff?"

"Come no closer. I will blow up this entire place. *Allah Akbar!* And you with it!"

"Don't want that to happen. I sure don't want to die. I'll bet you don't want to either. Right, buddy? What's your name? Mine's Remo."

"Do not play with me. Allah is against your kind."

"And I suppose you have a direct line to him. Well, I don't see Allah around here. What say we just talk this out?" Remo made a show of gesturing broadly with both hands. The terrorist's black eyes shifted back and forth between them. He didn't notice that Remo was creeping infinitesimally closer, taking microsteps.

"Why don't you tell me what this is all about?" Remo went on calmly. "Maybe I can help you."

"Either the *Shaitan* called Eldon Sluggard is brought here for punishment, or I will destroy this infidel shrine."

"Sluggard?" Remo asked. "Didn't he run for President last year?"

"I know nothing of that. *Est!* Stop! Come no closer!"

Remo obliged. He was very close to the terrorist now. But not close enough.

"Go! Go! Leave this place. Come back with Sluggard. I will negotiate no further. We demand *ghassas*, an eye for an eye!"

"Look, pal. . . ."

"*Ta kan na khor!* Don't move. See?"

And the terrorist opened his locked thumbs.

For a millisecond Remo froze.

"Ten-second fuse!" the terrorist shouted. "Ten seconds, and if I do not push the trigger back down, we all die!"

Remo moved then. He came in on a straight line, his hands like spearheads aimed at the crouching terrorist. He reached the man, slapped his hands apart, and in the split second when the detonator hung in the air, Remo grabbed it.

He jammed the detonator button down.

Then he felt the surge of electricity the detonator gave.

The terrorist's eyes went sick. "*Na! Na! Na!*"he cried.

"Oh, dog-doo!" Remo groaned. In an instant, he realized three things. The terrorist had lied about the detonator. The explosives were about to go off. And there was nothing he could do to save the Lincoln Memorial, never mind himself.

"Run for it, Chiun!" Remo cried. "I blew it!"

Dr. Harold W. Smith pressed the button that caused the computer terminal to drop into a well in his desk. He adjusted his Dartmouth tie, plucked the worn leather briefcase from his desk, and calmly walked from the office where he ran Folcroft Sanitarium, the cover for CURE.

He passed the guard at the door with a curt nod of recognition and, walking past his car, strolled over the immaculate lawn to the dilapidated docks that fronted Long Island Sound.

Mindful of his gray three-piece suit, Smith clambered aboard a worn rowboat, and taking up the oars, began rowing down the shore of Rye, New York. His briefcase lay at his feet.

When he reached a secluded inlet, he beached the rowboat and stepped out. Taking his briefcase, he walked a quarter-mile through uninhabited woods.

The helicopter waited for him in the clearing. Smith would have preferred to have the helicopter pick him up at Folcroft, but he had done that once already in the last year and it would raise suspicions if two military helicopters were forced down on the Folcroft grounds by "mechanical difficulties."

Smith stepped aboard without a word. The helicopter pilot sent the craft into the air. As far as he knew, Smith was a VIP he was shuttling to Kennedy International Airport on orders from the Pentagon. He had no inkling that no one in the Pentagon had initiated those orders. They had come from the lemon-faced man's computers to Pentagon computers and been relayed to an individual who had no idea where the instructions had originated.

As the helicopter clattered to Kennedy International and a waiting military plane, Smith opened the briefcase on his lap and booted up the portable computer it contained. He punched up certain files. The unit spat out photocopy-perfect laser printouts. Smith, because of the sensitive nature of his work, abhorred making hard copies of CURE materials, but he knew he would not be allowed to carry his briefcase into the FBI interrogation room. And he would need these documents if he were to succeed.

His one solace was that the paper was chemically treated so that within six hours the writing would fade untraceably.

In over twenty years of service in CURE, Dr. Harold W. Smith had never left anything to chance. He looked like the "before" segment of a laxative commercial, with his rimless eyeglasses and dry pinched features. His hair, as colorless as a weather-beaten New England fishing shack, had thinned out on top. His eyes matched the gray of his suit as if he had picked them out in the morning with his cufflinks.

He looked like a stuffy bureaucrat. The picture was true as far as it went. But it was also the perfect disguise for what Smith really was: the most powerful official in America.

FBI Agent John Glover mistook Smith for a district supervisor when Smith came down the twelfth-floor corridor of Washington FBI headquarters. His hands didn't even tighten on the grip of his Uzi machine pistol. Smith looked that harmless.

"Excuse me, sir," Glover said when Smith began walking up to him. "This is a restricted floor."

"I know," Smith replied. He flashed his billfold in

the man's face. John Glover saw the ID card. It bore
the seal of the Central Intelligence Agency. It indicated
that the man's name was Smith. Smith's thumb ob-
scured the first name and initial and Glover was about
to ask to see the card more clearly when Smith spoke
up in a stern voice.

"I'm here to see the prisoner. I assume he has not
yet talked."

"No, sir. He's a tough one. And you know the drill.
They never talk until the third day. Not without torture."

"We don't torture people in this country," Smith
said.

"No, sir. But maybe we should. Because of him a lot
of innocent people died."

"I understand your feelings, but I have to try."

Inwardly, FBI Agent Glover smiled. Who did this
old fart think he was? Even under standard FBI interrogation routines, with round-the-clock questioning and
sleep and food deprivation, the worst-trained profes-
sional agent usually held out until the third day. For
some reason, the third day was the breaking point.
They always talked then. But privately Glover wondered if this guy wouldn't go four days. He was tough.
Very tough.

"You'll have to leave your briefcase here," Glover
said.

"I have all I need with these papers," Smith said,
placing the briefcase on a nearby table. Smith had been
carrying the papers in the same hand that clutched the
briefcase. Just as he had carried his billfold in his other
hand as he stepped off the elevator. He was very thorough. In a high-security building like this, a man could
get shot for reaching into his pocket the wrong way.

"I'll have to pat you down," Glover said.

Smith spread his arms as the FBI agent frisked him.

"Okay, go in," Glover said. He pressed a button,
causing the door to unlock. Smith stepped in.

Less than a minute later, the FBI interrogation team came out, tight-faced and grumbling.

"What happened?" Glover asked.

"The officious bastard threw us out," he was told by the special agent in charge.

"Can he do that?"

"Some kind of national-security authorization. But I'll bet we can crack it. Come on, men. Let's work the phones."

FBI Agent Glover returned to his position, the Uzi cradled in his arms. He wondered if Smith would give it up before or after the FBI finished pulling strings.

It took nearly four hours. The FBI interrogation team had not returned. Agent Glover had been looking at his watch, making mental bets with himself over how much longer it would take for them to toss that CIA spook out of the building. Four hours seemed a long time, though.

Then the door behind him opened.

"Give up?"

"Yes," Smith said, his face grim.

"Tough?"

"More than most. You'd better get a stenographer in here. He's babbling like a child."

"Babbling?" asked Glover. He peered into the room. The terrorist was sitting at one end of a long table. His head was buried in his folded arms. His shoulders shook. At first Glover thought he might be laughing with hilarity at the expense of the gray-haired CIA bureaucrat who thought he could break him. But the muffled sounds coming from deep within him were not laughter. His face came up briefly as he wiped tears from the corners of his dark moist eyes.

"Christ! He's bawling his eyes out. What'd you do to him?"

"I talked to him."

"Talked?"

"It's very effective. Now I must go. My work is done."

"I don't believe this," Agent Glover said slowly.

"Has there been any word on the Lincoln Memorial situation while I was occupied?" Smith asked.

"Not that I—"

Then, through the thick walls of the FBI Building, came the cannonading of explosions. The walls shook.

"My God," Smith said. "They failed." And he hurried to the elevator, managing to move quickly without actually breaking into the indignity of a run.

7

Remo saw it in the terrorist's shocked eyes. They were both going to die. He grabbed the man by throat and crotch and backpedaled to the open air of the memorial steps. There wouldn't be time to get to all the explosive charges, but if he worked fast enough he could minimize the damage to the building. He only hoped Chiun had heard him in time to get clear.

On the steps, Remo spun in place three times. When he felt the momentum achieve its peak, he let go of the windmilling terrorist. The man shot up into the air. Remo raced back into the colonnade. He had severed the wires leading from the detonator, but that wouldn't matter now. The electricity was already sizzling along the wires. Remo was operating nearly as fast, but he knew it would not be fast enough.

He found a satchel leaning up against a far column. Remo scooped it up and sent it sailing. That was two. And so far no explosion. Would there be time to get to the third satchel? It was too much to hope for.

Remo scooted along the columns. Nothing behind any of them. He raced around the sanctuary. He knew it was not there. Maybe in one of the other rooms. Nothing in either of them. He raced to the side steps. They were clean too.

Where the hell was it?

Then he saw it. And his heart sank.

It was a leather valise. It dangled over the aged head of his mentor and trainer, Chiun. Chiun was holding it over his head triumphantly, so that Remo could see that he had found it.

Remo only had time to yell, "Chiun, get rid of that thing!" before the air filled with a series of explosions. Remo hit the hard floor and rolled into the shelter of Abraham Lincoln's feet. He shielded his face with his forearms.

The first concussive wave struck his eardrums. Remo opened his mouth in a soundless scream to equalize the pressure so his eardrums would not rupture. A second wave rolled over him. He waited for the third one.

When it didn't come, he raised his head and peered over his bare forearm.

The Master of Sinanju was standing over him, the valise held in both hands.

"Dud?" Remo asked dazedly.

"I would not say that. Others might. I would not. You are slow, even clumsy. But I would not call you a dud."

"I meant the explosives in that bag," Remo said, getting to his feet.

Chiun opened the valise and presented the contents for Remo's inspection.

"I know nothing of these devices. How can one tell if it is a dud?"

Remo looked into the valise. There was an electrical contraption fused with a claylike block of plastic explosives.

"It didn't go off?" Remo asked dully.

"Of course not. Why should it?"

"Because I pressed the frigging detonator by accident!" Remo shouted. "I felt the electricity go through the wires. Why did you think I was running around like a maniac, throwing the other charges into the air where they wouldn't hurt anything?"

"I thought it was one of your loud American holidays. You know, like the First of July."

"Fourth of July. And I did it to save our lives."

"How disappointing."

"That I saved our lives?"

"No," said Chiun. "That you did it in such a ridiculous way."

"I suppose you know a better way?"

"Yes."

"Prove it."

"Instead of throwing the explosives into the air where they could injure innocent birds, you might have pulled the wire from the other end. Like so." And Chiun displayed the opposite end of the detonating wire in one hand.

Remo looked at him uncomprehendingly.

"I don't get it," he said.

"It is the electricity that causes the ka-boom?"

"Right. There was no way to stop it. I felt the juice leave the detonator."

"And I stopped it from reaching the ka-boomer."

"You pulled the wire before the juice reached the charges?" Remo said in a dumbfounded voice.

"Was there a better way?" asked Chiun with an innocent face.

8

Once outside the FBI building, Harold Smith hailed a taxi and asked the driver to take him to the cheapest hotel in the District of Columbia that was still reasonably presentable. Smith named the hotel. Smith knew the name of every cheap but presentable hotel in every major American city. He prided himself on how much money he saved the taxpayers by his frugal habits.

The ride to the hotel took him within viewing distance of the Lincoln Memorial. With a barely repressed sigh of relief, Smith saw that the memorial was intact. The National Guardsmen were just picking themselves off the ground. Grit and metallic fragments were still drifting down from the boiling ball of smoke that hung over the building.

"Looks like the Guard saved the day," the driver called back.

"Concentrate on your driving, please," said Smith.

"Humph," the driver said, wondering who this stiff was, who didn't care whether or not the Lincoln Memorial was still standing.

Smith tipped the driver exactly thirty-seven cents for a five-dollar ride and registered at the hotel. They gave him a room in the back with a folding bed, and Smith immediately took the room phone off the hook so he would not be disturbed. He expected Remo to check in at any moment, but Remo would be calling on the special phone which Smith carried in his briefcase. In the meanwhile, there was work to do.

Smith set his briefcase on the scarred writing table and opened it. Seating himself like a student about to take a difficult test, he checked the portable phone unit to make sure the dial tone sounded. He replaced the receiver in the modem receptacle. It dialed a number automatically. Then Smith booted up the mini-computer. Working off the mainframe at Folcroft, the mini-computer accessed the true power of CURE—its vast data base. Compiled over the two decades Smith had run CURE, it was the ultimate information-retrieval center for information both important and obscure. What Smith's memory banks did not contain, Smith could access by infiltrating virtually any computer in the nation, from the Social Security files to any home computer that worked off the phone lines.

Smith keyed in a name and then hit the Control button. Instantly a column of text began scrolling. Smith digested the traveling data silently.

A blinking light indicated an incoming call. Smith hit the Pause button and picked up the receiver.

"Remo?"

"Who else? We saved the day."

"So I noticed," Smith said. He was still reading. His voice was crisp but preoccupied.

"There's something funny going on, Smitty. I think the hijacking in Honolulu was connected to this Lincoln Memorial thing. Both groups wanted a guy named Dullard."

"Sluggard. Reverend Eldon Sluggard," said Smith. "I'm reading a file on him right now."

"He ran for President last year, didn't he?"

"No, you're thinking of the Reverend Sandy Krinkles."

"Krinkles. Wasn't he the guy whose wife turned out to be—"

"No, that was another man entirely. But never mind that. I got Sluggard's name from the terrorist I interrogated."

"You broke him, huh?" Remo asked admiringly.

"Yes."

"What'd you use? Bamboo shoots under the fingernails?"

"No," said Smith.

When Smith did not elaborate, Remo said, "Hold on, Chiun is trying to say something. What's that, Little Father? Oh, yeah? Hey, Smitty, guess what? Chiun says his hijackers were asking about Sluggard too. What is this guy? Hostage of the month?"

"Reverend Eldon Sluggard is—or was—one of the most successful television evangelists in history. He's also the only one who so far has not been tainted by the series of scandals that have rocked that field. Why representatives of a foreign power want him so badly that they would virtually invade America is something we must find out. Please come to my hotel at once."

"What's the address?" Remo asked.

Smith gave it and hung up. He went back to work. Inwardly he was pleased that Remo and Chiun had saved the Lincoln Memorial, but the crisis was too pressing to waste valuable time. According to the terrorist Smith had broken, the government of the Islamic Republic of Iran wanted Reverend Eldon Sluggard, and wanted him badly enough to risk American retaliation. The crime, according to the terrorist, was making war on Islam, and in addition, sowing corruption on earth. Smith knew that the latter was a catch phrase used by the revolutionary courts to legally execute pro-Western Iranians and stone women judged insufficiently pious.

The terrorist had told Smith all that he knew. But it was meager and filled with generalities. Smith had wasted a full hour of the four-hour session with the man trying to pin him down on specifics. When the man began blubbering, Smith knew he was just a man taking orders, a fanatic without true facts. Still, what Smith had learned was vitally important.

A telltale light flashed in the margin of the computer

screen. Smith hit a key. It was the media-monitoring function. The system was alerting him that the name he had tagged for critical analysis, Reverend Eldon Sluggard, was right now holding a press conference that was being carried live by the news services.

Smith left the computer and turned on the room's television.

The overfed face of Reverend Eldon Sluggard, speaking in a Southern-fried Georgia accent, appeared on the screen. Sluggard wiped sweat off his lined brow with a handkerchief.

"Mah own theory, gentlemen," he was saying, "is that the mullahs in Ah-ran have finally shown their true anti-Christian colors. They have declared themselves to be enemies of Christianity. Because of mah vast influence and ministerial work abroad, they have targeted me as the man they must defeat before they can export their religious beliefs to this country."

"Is your TV show beamed into Iran?" he was asked by an unseen reporter.

"No, but Ah speak the word of the Lord, and it knows no national boundary or wavelength."

"Why do you suppose they attacked the targets they did and not your headquarters?"

"Ah suppose they didn't know where to find me. Ah don't broadcast mah address on TV, just a post-office box number."

"Has this anything to do with your reported fund-raising problems?"

"No," Reverend Sluggard said flatly. "Mah Cross Crusade fund drive is going to be a whoppin' success." He ran pudgy fingers through his heavily pomaded hair.

"You seem pretty sure of that. How do you know?"

"Because the Almighty revealed it to me."

"If he revealed that to you, as you claim, why hasn't he revealed the reason why Middle Eastern terrorists, allegedly in the pay of Iran, hijacked two aircraft, shot up an air show, and took the Lincoln Memorial hostage to publicize their demands that you be turned over to one of their Revolutionary Tribunals?"

"You'll have to ask him that," Reverend Sluggard said, wiping his beefy jowls. "All Ah know is that Judgment Day is a-comin' for America. If mah ministry falls to these fanatics, then none of you are safe. Ah'm callin' on all of America to join me and to get with God if they want this great Christian nation of ours to stand forever. For more information, tune into mah TV show, *Get with God*. Ah have all the answers."

"Reverend Sluggard—"

"That's all Ah got to say," Reverend Sluggard said, "but before Ah go, Ah want to reassure mah followers that the Lord's work will go on. No enemy of God will lay a hand on me or any of mah followers. Because Ah got this." He patted a thick leather-covered book. "And if you kind folks will allow, Ah want to read a passage Ah think appropriate to these troubled times: 'Though Ah be surrounded by serpents, Ah will fear no scoundrels. Though Ah stand in the quicksand of idolators, Ah know that the Chariot of the Lord is comin' to succor me and that his Hosts will raise their crossbows in mah defense.' Amen."

And slapping the great book closed, Eldon Sluggard walked off camera, leaving it to a network correspondent to explain that this was coming live from the Eldon Sluggard World Ministries in Thunderbolt, Georgia.

Smith stared at the screen, his brow knitting.

"There's no such passage in the Bible," he muttered.

Shutting off the television, he started for his minicomputer, when he heard a knocking at the door. He opened it.

"Remo. Master Chiun," Smith said without inflection. It was what passed for a warm greeting from Dr. Harold W. Smith.

"We appreciate your enthusiasm," Remo said, stepping in. He turned when he noticed that Chiun was still standing out in the hall, his back to Smith.

"You coming, Little Father?"

"I have not been formally invited in."

"I think he's still pissed at you, Smitty."

Smith cleared his throat. "Master Chiun, would you come in, please? I am sorry if I offended you."

"Wrong choice of words, Smitty," Remo whispered.

"If?" Chiun called over his shoulder loudly.

"That I offended you. Truly sorry. It won't happen again. And I wish you would come in. I have a question only someone with your knowledge of ancient history can answer."

Chiun immediately whirled in place. He marched into the room like an ancient vizier entering his king's inner chambers.

"I live to serve my emperor. What is your question?"

"Did they have crossbows during biblical days?"

"No," said Chiun as Remo closed the door. "The crossbow was a foolish invention of a later period. My ancestors first encountered it when—"

"Thank you, Master of Sinanju," Smith said abruptly. "That was all I desired to know."

Chiun's face tightened. His mouth pursed. His cheeks filled with indignity. He flounced around and again presented his back to Smith, his anger evident in his stiff posture.

"You did it again," Remo whispered.

"Later," Smith said. "I want you to listen carefully. The terrorists failed, but these people never give up. They will try again."

"Chiun and I are up to it," Remo said confidently.

"Speak for yourself, white man," Chiun asked. Remo ignored him. Smith continued speaking.

"We can't spend all our energies putting down terrorist attacks. There has already been loss of life. Whatever is motivating these people, they take the matter very seriously."

"You want us to go to Iran?" Remo asked.

Chiun suddenly turned, his face lighting with interest.

"It is the Persian New Year. The melons are quite good at this time of year," he said eagerly. "And Sinanju is well known to Persians—educated Persians. We could solve your problems with a few words whispered into the proper ears."

"No, I am not sending you to Iran," Smith said.

Chiun returned to presenting his back to his emperor.

"I want you two to look into Reverend Sluggard's ministry," Smith went on. "Find out why they want him. If we can uncover what is going on at this end, maybe we can expose or neutralize it. We might be able to reason with Iran. Speaking geopolitically, it remains in our interest to maintain a semblance of neutrality toward that country."

"You're dreaming, Smitty," Remo said tightly. "The U.S. and Iran are on a collision course. And will be as long as those religious crazies are running that country."

"Do not forget to mention the crazies running this country," Chiun muttered. "Some of them do not even bother to wear their crowns on correct occasions."

"What is he saying?" Smith asked Remo.

"I'll explain later. By the way, what's your hat size?"

"I'm not sure. I haven't worn a hat in thirty years. Why do you ask?"

"Long story. Okay, Smitty, we're on our way. By the way, where exactly are we going?"

"Sluggard's national headquarters are located in Thunderbolt, Georgia. It's outside of Savannah. Use false identification. Try to blend in with Sluggard's people. If we crack this quickly, we may beat the next wave of terror outbreaks."

"Gotcha, Smitty. You coming, Chiun?" Remo asked as he opened the door.

"I have not yet been given my leave by my emperor."

"You may leave, Master of Sinanju," Smith said quietly.

The Master of Sinanju turned softly, executed a polite but unostentatious bow, and floated out of the room, his bearded chin high in the air.

"I'll try to pull that wild hair out of his you-know-what before we get back, Smitty," Remo promised, winking.

9

Reverend Eldon Sluggard hurried from the auditorium of the Eldon Sluggard Temple of Tribute, under rows of moss-draped eucalyptus trees, past the quadrangle facing the Eldon Sluggard University, and entered the Eldon Sluggard World Broadcast Ministries Complex on the lazy banks of the Wilmington River.

"Get my media advisers, pronto," he snarled at a secretary, hurrying into a conference room.

When they arrived, moments later, the Reverend Eldon Sluggard was seated at one end of the long conference table, his hands resting on a thick leather volume with a gold-leaf cross embossed on its front cover.

The men, all dressed in sharp business suits, took their places. One of them switched on a cabinet television and popped a videocassette into a wall slot.

"Here's the replay, Reverend," he said as he took his seat.

The eyes of all thirteen men watched as the TV replayed the press conference of a few minutes ago. One by one the men began their critique.

"Good delivery there, El. You had 'em hangin' on your every syllable with that first bit about the mullahs tryin' to crucify America on a cross of oil."

"Nice comeback to that question about your finances. 'God don't count shekels in public.' But what's it mean?"

"Search me," said Reverend Sluggard, noticing that when his video image raised his left arm to gesture, a dark patch showed under his armpit. Sluggard lifted his arms and saw that the underarms of his immaculate white one-thousand-dollar Brioni suit were soaked with sweat. He scribbled a note to himself in the leather book to have his tailor reinforce the underarm padding. The man would bitch, as he always did. But screw him. The wop.

"Hold it. You see that part right there?" a consultant said. "Where you open up the Bible." He hit the Pause button of the remote control.

"Yeah? What of it?" Reverend Sluggard asked unhappily.

"You gotta be more careful, El. Look at that open page. You can almost see it. What if outsiders discovered that the Bible you carry has blank pages?"

"Who cares about outsiders? It's mah followers who count. And if they see me reading from a blank page, they'll declare it proof of mah godliness."

Everyone laughed nervously.

"And if they don't, you will, right, El?"

"Don't make fun of mah beliefs. Ah don't like it. Now, let's see the rest."

Eldon Sluggard watched as his TV image recited a passage and walked off camera. The tape stopped.

"Not bad. But you know, El, I don't think they had crossbows in Bible times."

"So what? Nobody reads the Bible anymore. They watch television. If they did read the Bible, someone would have noticed Ah make up all of my Scripture. They ain't. Not in the twenty years Ah've been in the God Game."

"Let's hope."

"So what do you men think? Did Ah cover mahself, or what?"

"You were slicker than spit, El. I think you got the media bamboozled. They're sure not going to be interviewing any ayatollahs for a dissenting opinion. And the American public wouldn't listen even if they did."

"One question, Reverend."

"Yeah?"

"How'd you rig it so that you got all this publicity? I mean, those terrorists acted like real ones."

"That's not your department."

"If you say so. But there are real folks dead out there. If you set this up and it gets out, it'll be like the Slim and Jaimie story, only worse."

"Don't mention those fairies in mah presence. What Ah want to know is, will this pull us through the next fiscal quarter?"

"Are you funnin' me? People are going to flock to give you money. The most fanatical, hated Islamic regime on earth has marked you for death. That's gonna get the little old ladies worked up from Tallahassee to Tulsa. It's gonna give your new Cross Crusade a happy boot in the ass. Work it right, and we could be golden again."

"Good. That's what Ah want to hear. You men are dismissed."

Silently the twelve media advisers filed out of the room, leaving Eldon Sluggard clutching his blank-paged Bible. His knuckles were white. A drop of sweat gathered in the vertical crease of his brow, rilled down the bridge of his nose, and spilled off the tip.

It had backfired. The whole thing. He must have been crazy to listen to that woman. Sure it had sounded good, but who would have thought it would come to this?

He reached out for the intercom. "Get me that Hoar bitch," he barked. Just wait until she showed. He'd fix her damned pew.

He waited. When the phone rang, he grabbed it, fumbled, and the receiver hit the floor. Reverend Eldon Sluggard got down on his hands and knees and hunted for the phone. He didn't get off the floor when he found it.

"Vic? That you?"

"El," a woman's breathy contralto voice said, and

Eldon Sluggard had to pull at his underwear to accommodate a sudden physiological reaction in his crotch. Damn that woman. She always did this to him. Even over the phone.

"We gotta talk," he said urgently.

"My temple or yours?"

"Mine. And don't joke at a time like this. Haven't you been watchin' the news? Ah don't dare leave this place. Those fuckin' ragheads want mah ass."

"Not as much as I do. I'm on my way. 'Bye."

"Bitch," muttered Reverend Eldon Sluggard, fumbling the phone back onto the hook. He got to his feet awkwardly. He felt his shorts rip.

"Damn that bitch," he repeated.

He sat down near his phone, trying to think of things that would cool his passion. He thought of cold showers but that only made him think of the last shower he had taken and who was with him in the stall. He tried thinking of his ex-wife, Griselda—as sure a cure as saltpeter—but her puffy face kept blurring and that of Victoria Hoar's, high-cheeked, long-haired, and topping a body as sinuous as a belly dancer's, kept intruding.

Then he thought about what would happen to him if Iran's fundamentalists got hold of him. They would chop off his hands first thing. They did that stuff over there to people who stole a moldy loaf of bread. Then they would cut off his feet. Then while they were looking for something else to cut off, they would get around to his manhood.

Just the thought of a bunch of bearded mullahs taking a sharp knife to his manhood gave Reverend Eldon Sluggard instant relief. And replaced it with sheer terror.

He began pacing the room, his handkerchief dabbing his face.

"Ah should never have listened to her. Ah should never have listened to her," he repeated endlessly, as if the very words were a charm that would ward off danger. "The bitch," he added.

Eldon Sluggard had not thought of Victoria Hoar as a bitch when he first met her. He had considered her the most infinitely desirable woman he had ever seen. That was at first sight. By the end of their first night together, he considered her his personal savior.

A great many people thought that the Reverend Eldon Sluggard believed in quite a different personal savior, but in truth, Sluggard believed in nothing. Except enriching himself.

Growing up in a tarpaper shack in Augusta, Georgia, Eldon Sluggard liked to tell people that even poor folks thought of his family as poor. His father ran a junkyard and sold scrap metal and old tires to make ends meet. He barely did at times. But he tried. He was a good man. Even Sluggard had to admit that. He was just dirt-poor. Eldon Sluggard knew that the Sluggards had been dirt-poor as far back as the Civil War. He, on the other hand, was going to be the first filthy-rich Sluggard.

He didn't know how. But one thing he was certain of: he wasn't going to work for it. His father had worked hard all his life and at forty he looked sixty, his skin all brown and wrinkled from the long hours in the sun, his hands so dirty from labor that even lye soap would not reveal their true color.

Eldon Sluggard got his first inkling of his future the summer he turned fifteen. A revivalist preacher came to Augusta and pitched his tent just down the road from his father's junkyard. It was the middle of summer and the tent promised relief from the heat and humidity, but mostly because admission was free, Eldon went in.

Eldon had never been to church in his life. The nearest one was too far to walk to, and although his father owned several cars, they were all up on blocks and missing critical parts. So it was all new to Eldon, this stuff about God. He had heard about God, of course. Who hadn't? Lots of folks in Augusta mentioned the Lord. Often by name. Usually it was after they hit their thumb with a hammer or found a chigger burrowing under their skin. Then they sang out the Lord's name real loud, they did.

The preacher in the tent also talked loudly of God. But he didn't use the Lord's name to curse. He used it to berate the people who sat meekly in the tent. And they took it. Every one of them. The preacher called them sinners. And they took it. He called them fornicators. And they sat in silence. Some winced. He called them undeserving of redemption—whatever that was— and they only sat there like so many dumb animals. A few sang out "hallelujahs" as if they agreed with the preacher.

And after an hour and a half of this abuse, with the men sweltering in the stifling air of the tent and the women waving their fans and adjusting their summer hats for the hundredth time, the preacher's men passed the plates.

Eldon Sluggard craned his neck to see what was in the plates. He thought the audience was going to be rewarded for enduring the preacher's abuse with sweets or ice cubes for their sweaty brows. But Eldon saw that the plates were empty.

Then the coins started clinking onto the plates. The folded bills flopped. People dug into their purses and wallets. And Eldon noticed that the poorer people in town seemed to give the most money.

It made no sense.

But when the plate came to him, Eldon saw it was heaped with bills and coins. And if anything made sense to Eldon Sluggard at the age of fifteen, it was money. Piles of it.

Because he had no money of his own, Eldon picked a quarter from the plate and let it drop back with a clink. While the people around him blinked at the sudden sound, he palmed a twenty.

Eldon Sluggard walked out of the revivalist tent, one fist clutching the bill in the security of his torn jeans pocket.

A heavy hand took him by the shoulder and hustled him around to the back of the tent.

"I saw what you did, boy."

Eldon looked up. It was the preacher. His voice was low, but the fire-and-brimstone quality was still there.

"Lemme go, mister. Ah ain't done nothing to you."

"You stole from the Lord, and I don't cotton to that."

"You got enough."

"Ain't no such thing as enough. You should know that. Look at you. I'll bet those clothes of yours would get up and walk if your daddy didn't lock the back door each night."

"You can talk. You got fine clothes."

"I earned these clothes, boy."

"You did not. You just shout at folks and insult 'em."

"And they pay me for that. You know why, son?"

"Because they're stupid."

"You're right close. Because they spend six days each week telling themselves they're good folks even while they go around sinning. I give 'em a little reminder that they ain't so wonderful. Then they go home feeling like they got something off their chests, made their peace with the Almighty by dropping an offering in the collection plate, and they go off fortified with the strength to sin some more."

"Don't make no sense to me."

"It's a funny world, son. But if you know how people are, you got 'em where you want 'em. It's called the God Game, and the best part of it is that anyone can play. Even you with your pimples and high-water pants."

"Can Ah keep the twenty?" Eldon had asked.

"Son, I just gave you a million dollars' worth of free advice. I think that's generosity enough. Now, fork over that twenty before I box your ears good."

Reluctantly Eldon Sluggard pulled his grimy hand from his dirty jeans pocket and slapped the crumpled twenty-dollar bill—the most money he had ever held in his hand—into the preacher's hand.

"You're mean," he growled.

"I get what's coming to me. Now, get your raggedy butt outta here, son. Maybe I'll see you in the God Game and maybe I won't. The choice is yours."

Eldon got. But he thought about the preacher's words all the way home. He asked his mommy for a dollar and she told him she had no money. Eldon called her a fornicator and an idolator, being sure to mention the Lord's name a few times, and then asked for the money again.

His mother turned from her pie-baking and looked at him with a sick white face. She ran out of the house and when his father charged back in, he was wearing his mean face and carrying his thick leather belt doubled in one hand.

Eldon Sluggard learned not to preach to his family that day. He tried preaching to his friends from a tomato crate by the side of the road. They laughed at him. He ran away later that summer. He could still feel that twenty-dollar bill in his hand.

Eldon hitchhiked south, finally winding up in Waynesboro, a lick south of Augusta. No one knew him in Waynesboro. He had figured out that if you're going to preach hell and damnation to folks, you get a lot more respect if you do it in someone else's backyard.

Eldon Sluggard's first tent was a big old hunk of cardboard suspended over four hickory sticks. It wasn't much, but after the plate got passed around—it was a foil pie plate from a store-bought apple pie—there was nearly twenty-eight dollars in it. Enough for a room. The next night there was thirty-two dollars, enough for a little tent. He had a real tent and two helpers inside of two months.

From there it grew. Eldon bought himself a Bible. He had never learned to read, so he made up his Scripture. It was easy. As long as he didn't quote from Mark or John or Luke or any of the books real preachers used, no one ever noticed.

The Eldon Sluggard empire grew like a snowball rolling down the highest peak in the Himalayas. It was unstoppable. When he felt he'd milked a town dry, he moved on. By the time he had hit every city in the Bible Belt and had to start over, a new flock had grown up, just as eager for salvation. And fleecing.

Eldon Sluggard got into television in 1968, when he noticed that he encountered fewer and fewer itinerant preachers during his travels. He found one driving a mobile home down Route 66 near the town of Garth, Mississippi.

"Hey, brother, tell me," Sluggard hailed. "We got the whole field to ourselves now?"

"Reckon so," the preacher said. He was old and losing his teeth. "Most of the young ones are in television nowadays."

"TV? You don't say. What're they doin' on TV, sellin' toothpaste for God?" And he laughed.

"Nope. They're raking in the shekels, same as you and me. Only they talk to a camera and ask folks to mail in the checks. Then they hire pretty girls to open the mail and run off to the bank. Where you and I are making thousands, they're accumulating millions."

"If that's so, brother, why ain't you gettin' your rightful share?"

"Because I like to look 'em in the eye when I take 'em. What's your excuse?"

Eldon Sluggard didn't have one. He pulled over at the next roadside motel in Biloxi and turned on the television.

The air was full of them. There was Quinton Schiller's Church of Inevitable and God-Ordained Apocalypse, Slim and Jaimie's 69 Club, and many others. Flipping the channels, he found that afternoon television was choked with them. On one channel he recognized the preacher who had first told him about the God Game. The guy was standing there with a microphone in his hand and tears streaming down his eyes. He was pleading with the unseen audience to send in their donations, or the ministry of the Reverend Lex Lumbar would be out of business in a month and the starving children of Biafra would all die.

Eldon Sluggard privately doubted that the evangelists claiming to be pumping money into Biafra and Bangladesh and all the other third-world countries were really sending anything to the little children who walked around naked with flies clinging to their faces and their stomachs sticking out like so many pregnant Pygmies. But hearing the anguish in the preacher's voice, Eldon Sluggard smelled blood. If Lumbar was in so much trouble, maybe he could buy the guy out.

When Eldon Sluggard located the offices of the Lex Lumbar World Ministries, he expected to find a shabby little place. But it was like the palace grounds of Monaco. He walked the manicured quadrangle, marveling at the Lex Lumbar University, the Lex Lumbar Broadcast Ministry—there was even a Lex Lumbar Memorial Hospital, and the bastard wasn't even dead yet!

Eldon Sluggard wandered into the broadcast building. No one paid him any notice. He was walking past a glassed-in broadcast studio when he recognized Lex Lumbar himself, looking older, more prosperous, and noticeably better-fed.

The man was standing in front of a painted backdrop of a desert. Beach sand covered the floor. The preacher wore a pith helmet, jodhpurs, and a pained expression on his face. Two little brown children sat at his feet. He held a third in his arms. The one in his arms had his eyes closed, and his head rested against Reverend Lumbar's chest. His arms and legs were lengths of bone with dried skin covering them. Lex Lumbar juggled the child in his arms and the baby barely moved.

"I've come all the way to Africa," the Reverend Lex Lumbar read off cue cards while the camera dollied in on him, "to show the plight of these poor starving infants. This poor child in my arms is near death. Won't

you help now? Send your check for twenty-five, fifty, or
one hundred dollars to the address on the screen. If it
gets here in time, I'll personally see to it that this little
feller gets some food."

"That's a cut," a director shouted. "Print it."

"About damn time," Reverend Lex Lumbar said angrily. He dropped the baby on the floor. It hit like a
two-by-four and just lay there. He walked over the
other two. "I need a drink."

Eldon Sluggard saw from the broken arm that the
dropped child was a wood-reinforced dummy. The two
on the floor were real.

"And get those pickaninnies back to their mothers,"
Reverend Lex Lumbar called back. "And be sure you
pay them good. I don't want this coming back to haunt
me," he said.

"Remember me?" Eldon Sluggard asked, following
him down the hall.

"No. Did I fire you once?"

"Ah tried stealing from you when you were a tent
preacher."

Reverend Lex Lumbar turned. "Yeah, I remember
you now. You took to the business. I know. I watch my
competition. Not that you are that anymore. This is the
electronic age. Tent preachers are pikers now. So what
do you want?"

"Ah came to buy you out."

"You and your grandmother between you couldn't
manage it."

"But Ah heard it over the TV that you're at your
rope's end."

"Take a look at this suit, boy. You think a man at the
end of his string is gonna wear threads like these?"

"It's a scam, isn't it?"

"And you ain't?"

"But this, it's so . . . so—"

"Lucrative. That the word you're reachin' for? Lucrative?"

"Take me on," Eldon Sluggard said quickly.

"What's that you say?"

"Take me on. Show me the ropes. You told me stuff before."

"You want a lot for your twenty dollars, don't you, boy?"

"Ah'm not a boy anymore."

"And you're not in my league, either. But I'll tell you what. You work for me five years for nothing and it's a deal."

"Five years?"

"Don't tell me you ain't built up a stake of your own."

"Yeah, but. . . ."

"Live off that."

"But—"

"Take it or leave it," said Reverend Lex Lumbar, starting off.

Eldon Sluggard looked around him. Everywhere he saw a building with a man's name on it, but it wasn't Lex Lumbar's name he was seeing. It was his own. He ran after the man.

"Deal," he panted, offering his hand.

"Five years." Reverend Lex Lumbar grinned, taking it.

But it didn't take five years. Eldon Sluggard wrested away control over the Lex Lumbar World Ministries after barely three. He did it only after he had learned everything possible about proselytizing over television. He could have forced Lumbar out within six months, which was as long as it took to learn his weaknesses, especially his predilection for call girls. That was how he did it in the end, by exposing the man as a charlatan and a sinner.

When all was said and done, he bought out Lex Lumbar for three cents on the dollar.

And thus was born the Eldon Sluggard World Ministries, which took in eighty million dollars a year for twenty fat wonderful years.

Until the great shakeout.

It started slow. First there was the phenomenon known in TV evangelical circles as the Great Grandma Crunch. Donations began slowing. At first it was dismissed as a blip in the donation curve. But the drop-off continued. The Dissemblers of God Evangelical Alliance was formed to look into the matter. It turned out that every religious network and program was affected by the same mysterious dwindling of donations.

The Alliance commissioned extensive polls. What they found sent a shockwave through the industry. The little old ladies—the backbone of TV evangelism—were dying off. It was a demographic thing. There just weren't enough older women with religious convictions left to feed the voracious appetites of the TV preachers. And it would be a long time before the baby boomers hit sixty.

With fewer of the faithful to feed the machinery, the TV evangelists began feeding on one another. Internecine warfare broke out. Brother accused brother of irreligious behavior on nationwide TV. The Charismatics denounced the Southern Baptists. The Pentecostals ridiculed the fundamentalists. And everyone jumped on the Catholics. Who jumped right back. The Dissemblers of God dissolved in nightly installments broadcast on the six-o'clock news.

It was a spectacle, transformed into a circus when, seeing the walls close in, the Reverend Sandy Krinkles jumped into the presidential race. He frightened middle America, but no segment of society panicked more than the other TV evangelists, who considered the prospect of one of their own in the White House as the kiss of death. The media attention alone, with the resulting IRS investigations and background checks, would have put them all in jail before it was over.

Then the bodies started to fall.

The Reverend Moral Robbins, seeing himself on the verge of bankruptcy, announced to the world that God was going to send everyone outside of his immediate family to hell if they didn't contribute fifty dollars a week to his show until the year 2012.

Dr. Quinton Shiller, while proclaiming that the judgment day was at hand before an open-air congregation, was struck by what was later identified as a meteor and squashed flat.

Slim and Jaimie Barker, while fighting off a hostile takeover from the Reverend Coyne Farewell, were revealed to be, not man and wife, but homosexual lovers. And the true symbolism behind their 69 Club came out.

And Reverend Sandy Krinkles, forgetting that he was no longer addressing a bussed-in studio audience of his Hour of Giving, told a skeptical group of voters that if elected President, he would outlaw the satanic ritual called Halloween and replace prime-time television programs with biblical reenactments. His bid for the presidency collapsed overnight, as did the waning support for his cable TV network.

And on the sidelines, untouched by scandal but suffering guilt by association, was the Reverend Eldon Sluggard.

"How bad is it?" Reverend Sluggard had asked his media advisers only three months before.

"I think you'd better fold your political-action group, the Moralistic Mass. Folks don't cotton to us being in politics no more."

"Done," said Reverend Sluggard.

"And the very word 'evangelist' is a no-no from now on. We suggest you call yourself a religious television personality."

"What's the difference?"

"If you let the media call you an evangelist, the average American will dismiss you as a political kook, a ripoff artist, a whoremonger, or gay, depending on which of your brethren is in the headlines that day."

"Don't call those bastards mah brethren. They've loused up a good thing for everybody."

"As a religious television personality you have a chance for survival."

"Give it to me in percentages. How much of a chance?"

"One in ten."

"Ah'm sunk," Reverend Eldon Sluggard groaned.

"Not if we launch a fast fund-raiser."

"Our last three fund-raisers only broke even."

"You got a better idea, El?"

Eldon Sluggard did not have a better idea. But he knew that he needed to raise over sixty thousand dollars a day just to keep his TV show, *Get with God*, on the air. And so he launched the first Eldon Sluggard Cross Crusade.

After two months, he called in his media advisers.

"How we doin'?"

"At this rate," he was told, "we're out of business by July."

"Any options?"

"We've drawn up a list of old folks—mostly women—who have put you in their wills as an act of faith."

"Yeah?"

"If they should—if something should happen . . . Well, you know, El."

El knew. He just didn't want to say it aloud. No telling which of the other preachers had the place bugged.

"How much we talkin' here? Round numbers."

"Maybe twenty million. Enough to keep us afloat until things settle down."

The Reverend Eldon Sluggard dismissed his advisers. Fleecing the elderly was one thing. Knocking them off was another. It wasn't that he was squeamish. A man who accepts the checks of people on welfare and the poor—which was the demographic group that *Get with God* appealed to—had no cause to cringe from any tactic. It's just that Eldon Sluggard wanted to figure out a foolproof escape plan if the law got involved.

Reverend Eldon Sluggard was considering what he

would do when he was buzzed that a visitor was here to see him. A visitor called Victoria Hoar, he was told.

He started to say, "Not today," when she stepped in.

She was tall and slim-hipped and pert-busted and everything that his ex-wife Griselda was not. She put out a tapered hand and instinctively Reverend Eldon Sluggard took it.

She smiled. And for the first time, Eldon Sluggard started having trouble keeping his attraction from showing through his trouser fabric.

"You have a problem, Reverend Sluggard," Victoria Hoar said coolly. "And I believe I can solve it."

"You can? You mean here and now?"

"Not quite that quickly or easily, I'm afraid."

"Oh," said Reverend Sluggard, his hand freezing on his fly.

Victoria Hoar looked down at the bulge of Reverend Sluggard's crotch and gave him an assured smile.

"Perhaps that problem too."

And before he knew what was happening, she had led him out of the building to his two-hundred-foot yacht, which was down in the books as the ministry's floating chapel, and to his personal stateroom, and to his four-poster bed.

"How'd you know Ah sleep here?" he asked as he kicked off his shoes. Victoria Hoar was undoing her brassiere. It was the kind that clasped in front. Eldon Sluggard had a weakness for that kind of bra.

"The same way I know a lot of things," she said, unzipping her skirt. Eldon Sluggard was so captivated by the way she undressed herself that he stared dumbfounded, forgetting that he was in the middle of unbuttoning his shirt.

"Yeah? Like what?" he asked.

"Like you've been divorced for almost a year and you don't dare date because of who you are and how much money you're worth. You can't remarry because your alimony is one of the contributing causes to your minis-

try's financial problems." She folded her skirt neatly
and laid it across the back of a chair. Eldon liked that.
Most women didn't have the presence of mind. They
usually let their clothes drop to the floor. "And that
you've been as horny as a ram since your wife divorced
you."

"Since before that. She got fat. The bitch."

"Some women do when they get to her age."

"She could have warned me. It was in her damn
genes." Eldon's voice trailed off. The panties were coming down, crisp and white. They joined the skirt on the
chair, and Victoria Hoar, walking like Belit through a
Cecil B. DeMille film, joined him on the bed.

"You seem to know a lot about me," he muttered.

"Almost everything. Now let me help you finish un-
dressing and later we can talk about my ideas to rescue
your ministry."

"Just a minute," said Eldon suddenly, his eyes coming into focus. "Ah forgot something."

Eldon Sluggard hopped off the bed and got down on
his hands and knees. Taking a heavy flashlight, he
shone it under the bed.

"It's okay," he said, getting back on the bed. "There's
no one under the bed."

Victoria Hoar arched a penciled eyebrow. "Spies?"

"No," replied the Reverend Eldon Sluggard, climb-
ing on top of her cool immaculate body. "The devil."

It was in that first twenty minutes of bliss that Eldon
cried out that Victoria Hoar was his personal savior—
and she hadn't even revealed her master plan yet.

Pacing his conference room, the afterimages of that
first fevered night together fading in his mind, Eldon
Sluggard wished that he hadn't. The woman was great,
but no piece of tail was worth being drawn and quar-
tered by Moslem fanatics. And where the hell was she?
He was going to tell her off. This was it. This was quits.

Victoria Hoar entered the room with the assurance of
a woman to whom no room, no building, was off-limits.

"This is your fault!" Eldon Sluggard thundered in his best orator's voice, turning on her with an accusing finger.

Victoria Hoar looked down at his crotch with a knowing smile. "Is it now?" she asked.

The Reverend Eldon Sluggard looked down at himself. His zipper was becoming undone. It looked like magic. But it was only the pressure of his manhood straining to burst free. Damn, he thought, I shouldn't have thought of that first night.

"Forget this!" Sluggard shouted, pointing to himself. "That isn't me. That's just the flesh, and the flesh is weak. Not me. Ah'm strong. Ah'm fortified with the word."

Victoria Hoar clicked over to his side, picked the heavy book off the table, and laid it in his hands so that it fell open. The open pages showed as white as snow.

"Hallelujah!" she said smugly.

"This can't go on. Have you been reading the papers? Do you know who's gunning for me? What they'll do?"

"Forget today's problems. We have to concentrate on tomorrow's opportunities," Victoria Hoar said, her face inching toward his, her perfume billowing into his nostrils, her hands kneading his hips, moving in growing circles, so close but not quite in the right place.

"Forget?" he said weakly, dreamily. "How can I forget?"

And Victoria Hoar's moist mouth touched his briefly, her tongue darting between his teeth, and then she sank to her knees and her tongue began to work in earnest and Reverend Eldon Sluggard forgot all about the terrorists with their AK-47's and the mullahs with their sharp instruments.

He forgot everything.

10

Rashid Shiraz trembled as he entered the great Parliament building in downtown Tehran. He was not used to trembling. For nearly a decade he had made others tremble, for he was one of the most brutal of Iran's Revolutionary Guard. But he had never stood before a Grand Ayatollah before. Nor had he had any truck with Supreme Defense Commander General Adnan Mefki. The Pasdaran despised the Iranian military. The military hated the Pasdaran. Everyone hated the Pasdaran.

But Rashid Shiraz understood in the early days of the Revolution that he who did not hold power during the transition was unlikely to hold on to his head.

Rashid had been nothing under the Shah. A beggar in the streets of Tehran, a thief who eluded the police, and later, as his crimes grew bolder, the dreaded Secret Police called SAVAK. When the Ayatollah Khomeini returned from French exile, the executions began immediately. Rashid had just lifted a businessman's wallet when he ducked around a corner. He saw a bearded mullah exhorting Revolutionary Guards to hang a trio of schoolteachers who had been accused of counterrevolutionary deeds. They were made to stand on old Coke cartons as nooses were fitted around their necks. The mullah himself kicked the cartons from under their feet. The makeshift scaffolding collapsed. In a fury, the mullah personally shot the accused as they lay in heaps.

It was then that Rashid fully understood the true meaning of the phrase "dog eat dog," and he knew that all of Iran was about to become a feeding ground. And who better than Rashid Shiraz to play the role of chief cannibal?

He joined the Pasdaran. It took nothing to join, other than a willingness to shout slogans, pay lip service to Allah, and carry out brutal and merciless orders.

With rifle in hand, and men under his command, Rashid Shiraz began paying back old grudges. The jeweler who turned him in for stealing was denounced as pro-Western. He was shot before a firing squad. The woman who spurned his advances was buried up to her neck and stoned to death. The landlord who had thrown him out one cold winter for not paying his rent was pulled from his fine house in the Doulat quarter. The house and all its contents became the property of Rashid Shiraz.

Rashid Shiraz came to live like a king in Tehran while the old rulers drowned in their own blood. It had gone well for him, even during the bitterest days of the war with Iraq, when, as section after section of the city was turned to rubble by enemy rockets, Rashid abandoned the home that he had acquired and agreed to a transfer to the Kharg Island oil facility. A house was offered for his use, but it was too small. He walked the street with his pistol hanging from his tight fist until he found one he wanted. He knocked on the door. When a woman, veiled in the traditional *chador*, answered, he tore the veil from her face, and firing several shots into the air, denounced her as an adulteress and then shot her husband when he came to her aid.

To the gathering crowd, he pronounced the couple to be *Mufsed fel-Ardh*, Corrupters of the Earth, and after they were hauled off for summary disposal, took the house as his. It was as easy as that in revolutionary Iran.

But now Rashid Shiraz trembled. He understood better than anyone that in a land where bitter men in turbans could justify imprisoning or killing anyone merely by quoting passages from the Koran, no one was truly safe. Not even a Revolutionary Guard. The tide had a way of turning against any man who did not watch his back. Who was to know that some relative of one of his victims did not come to power and demand Rashid's head? When Rashid heard that he had been summoned to go before a Grand Ayatollah and a general, he thought he had angered someone too powerful even for him to deal with.

Retainers greeted him at the entrance and in silence brought him to the Ayatollah's modest quarters.

"*Salaam,*" said Rashid Shiraz, placing one hand dutifully over his heart, his head inclining in the traditional gesture of respect and humility.

The Ayatollah sat on a rug on the otherwise bare floor. The black turban which signified direct descent from the Prophet sat heavily on his head. He raised his hand in a gesture of greeting that was so indolent as to appear feeble. The general stood off to one side, his face glowering. Rashid Shiraz' bitter heart quailed.

"*Salamm alechim,*" the Grand Ayatollah whispered.

"May Allah maintain your shadow," Rashid Shiraz said deferentially.

"And yours," the general said. But his eyes spoke volumes of distaste.

Rashid Shiraz regarded both men in the lengthening silence. The Ayatollah looked the very image of holiness, but Rashid knew that the mullahs, repressed for so long under the Shah, and his father before them, had soured on life. No kindness existed in their breasts. It was said that they hennaed their beards with the blood of their victims. Rashid—who had no love for their religious beliefs any more than he had for the West's— did not know that as a fact, but he did know that hundreds of thousands of Iranian mothers were in mourning because the mullahs preferred to martyr their children rather than submit to a negotiated peace with Iraq until the war was nearly lost. In the aftermath of their folly, Iran was crumbling, and the formerly laughable counterrevolutionary National Liberation Army had replaced the Iraqis as the thorn that could not be withdrawn. And still the mullahs made pronouncements and urged the populace to fight on.

Even Rashid Shiraz had grown weary of it. But as long as he was not ordered to the front, he kept his opinions to himself.

"You are the one who uncovered the foul Western plot against us," the Grand Ayatollah said softly. His words escaped his beard like ants fleeing a hole in a rotted tree.

"Yes, Imam," Rashid admitted.

"We have interrogated this Cross-Worshipper. This *koffar* told us that a king among Cross-Worshippers, a man very powerful in America, is behind this plot against Islam."

"Death to the Cross-Worshippers!" Rashid shouted automatically. He shut up when General Mefki signaled for him to contain his zeal.

"This unbeliever is known as Reverend Eldon Sluggard," the Ayatollah droned on. "The word 'reverend' denotes holiness in America, but we know how godless those people are."

"This man must be punished," said Rashid Shiraz firmly, but quietly. General Mefki nodded. Rashid regarded him carefully. This was not going in the direction he had feared. Perhaps he was safe after all. But he noted how well-fed the general looked. He had the look of a *timsar*, a pre-Revolution general. Perhaps he continued to harbor pro-Western designs. Rashid told himself that it would serve him well to learn this man's background. Perhaps he had a fine house that would be good to live in.

"It is good you agree," said General Mefki directly. "For we believe you are the one to undertake this task."

"How? I will do anything."

The general fingered his tiny mustache with satisfaction, and Rashid knew him then as a former officer of the Shah, probably a homosexual too. Almost every officer was a homosexual in the days of the Shah. It was part of their corruption.

"We have sent agents to America to take this man Sluggard. Although you will not read of it in the newspapers, these attempts have failed. Our complaints to the international community are met with scorn and derision. Evidently this Sluggard is so powerful that he sways international opinion, or—"

"Or he is in the pay of the American hypocrites," the Grand Ayatollah put in. "If so, this is another black mark against *Shaitan Bozorg*, the Great Satan, and must be punished."

"Let us sink their warships in the Gulf!"

"You are forgetting what happened the last time we tried that," General Mefki said dryly. "No, what we have in mind is more direct. Our attempts to force America to hand this Sluggard over to us have failed. Now we will try another way."

And before the next words came, Rashid Shiraz felt dizzy. He did not hear the words when they came. There was a roaring in his ears and his breathing came hot and bitter. He did not hear them order him to America to assassinate Eldon Sluggard. He did not have to.

When they revived Rashid Shiraz with smelling salts, even before his head cleared, his mouth was volunteering him for service on the battle front. Even deadly poison gases were preferable to what he was being asked to do.

He came to in a hospital. General Mefki loomed over him. There was no sign of the Grand Ayatollah.

"You are going to America," the general said. He touched his mustache and then Rashid realized it was not some leftover effete gesture, but that the general was attempting to mask a self-satisfied smile. No one hated the Revolutionary Guard more than the generals—because the Pasdaran answered to no one and had usurped the military's primacy everywhere.

"But it is a foul and corrupt place, full of sin and unbelievers. They eat pork. Their woman show their brazen faces in public. Their priests do not wear beards. Surely Allah does not ask a True Believer to enter such a perdition?"

"Since when are you a True Believer, thief?" the general answered openly. "And we are not asking you to live there. Take the American with you. He will guide you. He is so frightened and so desperate to return to his homeland that he will commit any crime to see America again."

"I would rather go to the front with the *bassejis*," said Rashid Shiraz sincerely.

"The war effort needs volunteers, and nothing would please me more than to see you facing an enemy who shoots back. But the Grand Ayatollah has decreed this. So you will go."

Lamar Booe cursed the darkness.

Prayer had not worked. Faith had not worked. God refused to hear him. And the darkness of the stone cell continued unrelieved. Even when they brought bowls of soupy water, no light penetrated his cell in the basement of Tehran's Evin prison. They kept him in darkness to break him. But he had already broken. He had told them everything. And he was ashamed.

At first, he blamed himself for not having enough faith. But the Reverend-General had promised that he would be safe from harm so long as he held the banner of the Cross Crusade high. God would watch over him. He was a lamb of God. A lamb with a proud banner. After they extracted the truth from him, they put him in the cell with its Turkish-style toilet—a square hole over an open sewer, with things crawling over his feet when he squatted over it—and Lamar resolved that he would be stronger when they returned to interrogate him further.

They did not return. And the soupy bowls continued to come and the stench continued to waft into the dripping limestone cell and the darkness continued unabated.

Lamar cried out in anger at the darkness, at the Reverend-General, at the Lord. It was all a lie. A lie. And he had believed it.

The guards heard him wail, first in bitter English and then in a spiraling incoherence. They laughed cruelly. In English they taunted him. "Your God has forsaken you, American. If you desire mercy, you must ask Allah. You are in Allah's land now. How do you like it, American devil?"

Through the walls, dimly, distantly, came words being shouted. Only their monosyllabic monotony indicated the passage of time. If the crowd were chanting, it was day. If not, night. But it was always night in the cell.

The shouting was a blind repetition of the same words, over and over.

Marg bar Amrika! Marg bar Amrika!

Death to America, was the cry. It continued so long and so monotonously that it was like a catchy song that stayed in the mind until you grew to despise it. It was the same chant that haunted the ears of the American hostages throughout their long 444 days of captivity in Iran. And they were diplomats and guests of the country. Lamar Booe was a confessed invader and spy.

After an unknown length of time, Lamar Booe found himself whispering it under his breath. Chanting it along with the crowd. Not that he believed it, but the chanting was his only human contact, and joining the chanting was his only link with humanity and sanity.

"*Marg bar Amrika! Marg bar Amrika!*" Lamar Booe whispered. The tears ran hotly down his soiled cheeks.

The chanting had ceased for the day when the oaken door to his cell opened. This time, a light came with it.

Lamar cried out, the pain to his eyes was so intense. He covered his eyes with his hands.

A man knelt beside him, putting down a kerosene lantern. He grasped Lamar's longish hair in his hand and pulled his head back. With his other hand the jailer forced Lamar's eyelids open.

"Look, look, Cross-Worshipper. Behold the light of Allah. If you cannot endure it, it will burn your eyes from the sockets of your very skull."

"Leave me alone," Lamar said resignedly. "I want to go home. I want my parents."

"And we want this unholy holy man, Eldon Sluggard," the voice hissed. "You do not know me, Cross-Worshipper, but I am the one who saved your life on the oil tanker. I knocked you into oblivion. I kept you alive. Now I will do you another favor."

"I wish you had killed me," Lamar Booe moaned, the light seeping past his eyelids. It was red. Everything was red. But the pain was lessening.

"I will take you back to America. Back to Sapulpa, Oklahoma. You would like that, Lamar Booe?"

"Please."

"I will take you back, only if you lead me into this den of serpents where this Sluggard dwells."

"Why?"

"So that he will face his just punishment. He tricked you into invading the Islamic Republic of Iran. Now he has abandoned you. Do you not want to see him punished?"

"Yes," Lamar Booe sobbed. "I hate him with all my might."

"Not as much as I do," said Rashid Shiraz, yanking Lamar Booe to his feet and hauling him from the cell.

11

The Reverend Eldon Sluggard had collapsed into his conference-room chair like a deflated balloon. His broad face was flushed with release. He watched Victoria Hoar quietly and expertly reapply the reddest lipstick he had ever seen to her moist mouth. Just watching that mouth redden got him going all over again.

Someone knocked at the door.

"Who is it?" Sluggard asked, placing his mock Bible on his lap so that his recurring problem didn't show.

"Head of security, Reverend Sluggard."

"Come in."

A man built like two linebackers welded side by side stepped into the room.

"Yeah?" Sluggard asked, wiping his face. Victoria Hoar retreated to a corner of the room and pretended to examine a bookcase.

"There are two men at the gate, Reverend Sluggard. They say they can solve your security problem."

"Do Ah have a security problem?" Sluggard asked.

"Not that I'm aware of."

"Yes, you do," a squeaky voice said.

"What is that?" Sluggard asked, clutching the Bible in his lap.

The security chief looked around, as if for a hidden loudspeaker.

"Your security problem," a deep male voice said. A different voice.

"That sounds like the two I mentioned," the security

chief said frantically. "But they're being held at the gate. How can they be here?"

"Obviously, there is a security problem," Victoria Hoar said coolly. Her eyes darted from Sluggard to the security man.

"Don't just stand there like an oaf," Sluggard shouted. "They're in this room. Find them!"

The security chief crashed around the room desperately. It was a rectangle furnished only with the conference table and chairs. The walls were all bookcases and TV monitors. There was no place one person could hide, never mind two of them. The security chief flailed around the room anyway, his hands running over the walls, as if seeking a secret door.

"You're getting warmer," the deep male voice taunted.

"No, colder. He is getting colder," the squeaky voice said querulously.

"Be fair, Little Father. Don't make it any harder for him."

Victoria Hoar stepped away from the roaming security chief. "Where could they be?" she asked sharply. "There's no possible hiding place."

"Never mind that. What I want to know is how long have they been here?" Eldon Sluggard's face was desperate. He was seeing his name on the cover of next week's *National Enquirer*.

"We came in with the uniformed side of beef," the deep voice offered.

"Impossible!" Victoria retorted. "He came in alone."

"Dammit, man!" Sluggard raged. "Find those two! They're making an idiot of you!"

The security chief, his face reddening, pulled a .357 Magnum revolver out of a shoulder holster. His beefy fist made it look like a .38.

"Don't worry," he growled. "I'll get them."

He crashed around the room like a charging buffalo. Eldon Sluggard retreated to a corner. Victoria Hoar joined him. Panic was in Sluggard's face. Victoria's registered only a puzzled intellectual curiosity.

"They're not here," the security chief said after a thorough search. "It must be a trick. A radio transmitter or something."

"Try under the table," the squeaky voice suggested.

"Of course, under the table," the security guard said. He bent at the waist to look. And when he did, a lean man in a black T-shirt was revealed. He had been standing behind the security chief. He smiled.

"Hi!" he said.

An Oriental head stuck out from behind the lean man's chest. He waved a long-nailed hand.

"They're right behind you!" Eldon Sluggard howled.

The guard shot to his feet. "What?" he said. To Sluggard's horrified eyes it looked as if the guard was suddenly standing alone by the conference table. The two men had vanished the instant the security chief straightened up.

"Behind you!"

The guard whirled. He saw nothing.

Eldon Sluggard saw something entirely different. He saw the guard turn as if on a revolving plate. And as if set on the same plate, the two interlopers turned with him. Exactly, precisely with him, as if they knew his moves an instant before he did.

Now the security chief was staring frantically, the two men standing calmly behind him. The Oriental turned his head and with a mischievous expression laid a quieting finger before his lips.

"Where?" the guard wailed.

"Right behind you!" Sluggard howled.

"You said that. I don't see anyone."

"That was before," Sluggard cried. "Now they're where you were."

"Here?" asked the guard, turning. He waved his oaklike arms in the empty air in front of him, as if his quarry were invisible.

"They're gone." Eldon Sluggard gasped. For when the security chief had turned, the two had moved with him.

"Don't be silly," Victoria snapped. "They're behind him again. It's just that we can't see them. Watch and I'll prove it."

Victoria Hoar walked to the end of the room. The two were obviously skilled in some kind of advanced stealth tactics. Perhaps something like the old ninja warriors used. She knew that when she got to the other side of the quaking guard, they would be visible again.

They were not. For once, Victoria Hoar's composed features broke into shocked lines.

"They vanished!" she gasped.

"What did I tell you?" Sluggard said angrily.

"Where are they?" the guard cried. He acted like a man who had been told a thousand sniper rifles were being trained on him. He didn't know which direction to fear most.

"All right, you two. You win. Ah have a security problem. Ah admit it," Eldon Sluggard called.

The sound was like a tree being struck by lightning. Later, Eldon Sluggard swore he had actually seen the jagged flash in the conference room, but that was impossible.

But what all three occupants of the room later agreed to was that there was a loud crack, and when they stopped blinking, the conference table was falling in two long sections as neatly as if a buzz saw had been run along its length.

Standing between the two falling sections were the tall white man and the little Oriental. The Oriental wore a green robe that was decorated with yellow nightingales.

"Who . . . who are you?" Eldon Sluggard stammered.

"My name's Remo. Remo Cleaver. And this is Chiun. We're your new heads of security."

"Over my dead body," the former head of security barked.

He drew a bead on the Oriental's head. The Oriental whirled, his kimono swirling like a cheerleader's poodle skirt, and his hand swept out.

The security chief felt the impact on his weapon. It was a light touch, exactly the kind of a blow he would expect from a frail old man. Ineffectual.

Grunting a relieved laugh, he took aim again. The old Oriental simply retreated to a clear space and folded his arms into the wide sleeves of his kimono. The guard pulled the trigger.

Click.

Must have been a misfire, he decided. He pulled it again.

Click click click, went his .357 Magnum revolver.

"They couldn't all be misfires," he said stupidly. He went to break open the cylinder. It was then he recognized what the problem was. There was no cylinder. There was instead a square frame where the cylinder had hung.

"I believe this is what you seek," the old Oriental said, plucking the missing cylinder from a sleeve.

"Give it back," the security chief said hoarsely. Raising his weapon like a club, he charged the old man.

The Master of Sinanju shrugged. He flicked the cylinder away with a delicate finger. The cylinder flew across the room, caught the guard in the solar plexus, and carried him to the far wall. The wall TV set shattered and the security chief poured to the floor like so much melting taffy.

The old Oriental turned to the Reverend Eldon Sluggard with a serene expression on his wise face.

"We can discuss salary requirements later," he said.

"You're hired," Eldon Sluggard said quickly.

"Of course," said the Master of Sinanju, bowing. "One question, though."

"Yes?"

"Why me? Ah mean, why are you volunteering to help me out. Ah had—or thought Ah had—the finest security force money could buy."

"We heard about your problems with the Iranians," Remo told him. "We thought you could use our special skills."

"It was his idea," the old Oriental put in. "Remo was attracted to this task because of his newly rediscovered religious beliefs."

"Born again?" asked the Reverend Eldon Sluggard, smiling.

Remo gave the old Oriental a glancing frown. "You could say that," he admitted.

"Sometimes I think he was born yesterday," Chiun inserted archly.

"Well, then, welcome to God's country!" Reverend Eldon Sluggard said expansively. He put out a bejeweled hand. Remo shook it tentatively. Chiun pretended not to notice the gesture. Sluggard recovered quickly. "Victoria, why don't you show these fine folks to their quarters while Ah take care of that matter we discussed."

"My pleasure, Reverend Sluggard," said Victoria Hoar. She was not looking at Eldon Sluggard when she spoke. She was looking at the man who called himself Remo Cleaver. A dreamy smile alighted on her face.

"Don't be long, though," he said pointedly.

"Of course," Victoria Hoar said in a vague voice. "Absolutely."

Frowning, the Reverend Eldon Sluggard left the room. His muttered "bitch" floated in his wake.

12

The Reverend Eldon Sluggard stormed onto the set of his *Get with God* program. A skeleton crew of gaffers and camera operators was busy preparing for the next broadcast taping.

"You're early, El," said Win Jymorski, the show's director.

"Get everything together. Fast. We're taping another Cross Crusade spot."

"Now? I haven't seen the script."

"There's no script. Ah'll wing it. Ah'll show those ragheads in Tehran. They don't scare me!"

Quickly the electricians brought up the lights. The cameras moved into position. The soundman fussed with microphone levels.

And the Reverend Eldon Sluggard got up on the dais in front of a great flat map of the world. He picked a steel pointer off the Lucite podium. He paced impatiently, collapsing and expanding the pointer grimly.

Victoria was right. One setback wasn't going to knock Eldon Sluggard on his ass. That woman sure had a way of putting things in perspective. Especially when she got down on her knees.

"Whenever you're ready, El," the director called.

"Okay. Now," said Eldon Sluggard decisively. His voice dropped into a deeper register. It was his preaching voice. In the glory days of the Eldon Sluggard World Ministries, it used to make the over-sixty crowd swoon. But now Eldon Sluggard was targeting an entirely different demographic group.

"We're on," the director called, throwing a cue.

Eldon Sluggard faced the camera squarely. The red light came on. He smiled expansively.

"This is the Reverend Eldon Sluggard, and Ah'm speakin' to the youth of America. Yes, you. Don't reach out for the channel selector because it's not just me knockin', it's God. God Almighty, and your country."

Eldon Sluggard took a deep breath.

"You love your country. Don't you? And you want to see it strong. And you want to see it continue to be Christian. Well, Ah want that too. Hallelujah! But there's some who have designs on our sweet nation. Maybe you don't read the papers. Maybe your folks don't talk about this around the dinner table. And you know why? 'Cause they're scared too! That's right. Even as Ah'm standin' here talkin' at you, there are people in a foreign capital plotting to take over this country. No, it's not the Russians, bad as they are. It ain't the Chinese either. It's worse people. You've seen them on TV, talkin' out of both sides of their scrubby beards. You've heard how they once held our diplomats hostage for more than a year."

Sluggard pounded the Lucite podium with a fat fist.

"That's right. You know who Ah'm talkin' about. It's those mullahs in Ah-ran. You can see it on this here map."

Eldon Sluggard whipped the pointer in his hand like a car aerial. It jetted out its full length. He placed the point over the Persian Gulf. On the map, it was called the Pershing Gulf, but the camera wouldn't show that because the lettering was too small.

"This is Ah-ran," he went on. "The most brutal, repressive nation on earth. You see this gimcrack here? That's what they call a red crescent. It's got nothing to do with Communism. This is the symbol of the Moslems. Now the people in Ah-ran are Moslems. They ain't like

us. Not that Ah'm against Moslems, you understand.
There are good Moslems and there are bad Moslems.
You look around the Middle East here, and parts of
Africa, and you see a whole lot of these little red
crescents. Most of these other countries belong to the
Moslem world. But they belong to the Sunni Moslems.
Ah-ran belongs to the other kind, the Shiites. Now if
you have trouble keepin' 'em straight, Ah'll let you in
on a little trick. The Sunni Moslems are the good
Moslems. Ah kinda nicknamed them the sunny Moslems
on account of they're always happy and smiling. Now,
the other kind, Ah call the shitty Moslems on account
of them being assholes.

"Now you're probably askin' yourself, what's the Reverend Eldon Sluggard doin' usin' language like that on
TV, him a man of God and all. Well, Ah'll tell you. God
don't expect a Christian to take offenses lying down.
And Ah'm mad as hell. Ah have a hatred—a holy righteous hatred—against these shitty Moslems. Ah hate
them because of the hostages they took. Ah hate them
because they want to choke off the Pershing—er, Persian
Gulf, which is this hunk of water right here, and keep
us from getting our oil out. No oil, no cars. No cars, no
Saturday-night dates."

Reverend Sluggard paused to wipe his sweating brow
clean.

"But most of all, Ah hate these shitty Moslems because they ain't satisfied with Ah-ran. No, sir. They
want the whole damn world. They especially want America. They don't want us like the Reds want us. No, the
Russians, bad as they are, want to take our religion
from us. They want us to deny Christ. But these bad
Moslems, they won't be satisfied with that. No. They
want us to throw out our Holy Bibles and replace them
with their book, the Koran. They want all of us good
Americans to be Moslems like them. They want to turn
the clock back. You know all these good things you got?
Your music? Well rock-and-roll will be the first to go.

And you girls. You like your make-up? In Ah-ran, Moslem girls your age got to wear a veil. If you're pretty, you got to hide that fact. If you want to get married, you gotta sit around in a room until some Moslem guy picks you out. Then you gotta marry him. He could be as ugly as sin—and a lot of Ah-ranians are—but you gotta marry him anyway. That's the Moslem law, the law the mullahs in Ah-ran want to export to our Christian America.

"What's that, you say?" Reverend Eldon Sluggard said suddenly, cocking an ear to the camera. He fingered the ear forward.

"You don't believe it? You find this hard to swallow. Never heard of this stuff before? Well, you don't have to take Reverend Sluggard's word for it. You can look it up. That's right. These mullahs aren't just whisperin' these things among themselves. They've given speeches, big as life. They're callin' for a Moslem world, ruled by their ayatollahs.

Sluggard whipped his pointer out again.

"Look at this here map again. You see all these other countries? These ones with crosses on 'em? Those are the Christian countries. Lots of them, you say? Sure. Now. But what about in five years? In ten? Can you be sure Mexico won't become a Moslem country? Or Canada? And if that happens, what about us? It'll be too late to think about fightin' back when we're surrounded.

"Ah hear some of you laughin' out there. What have you got to laugh about? You settin' there in your comfortable homes with stereos and CD players. You got it soft. And the mullahs know it. They know you ain't got the faith. They know you're a soft target. Ah'll bet most of you don't go to church. Ah'll bet most of you wouldn't lift a *finger* to defend Christianity.

"Well, those of you who won't, why don't you get along with your having fun and your blind ways? Because Ah'm through talkin' to you milk-livered cowards. Ah want to talk to the smart ones whose palms are sweatin' at the sound of mah words. Ah'm directing mah words at the ones who are seein' red at the thought of those ragheads taking over this great free Christian land of ours. Ah'm talking to you! Are you afraid? Well, you oughta be. You oughta be terrified. Ah know Ah am. Sometimes. Ah've been warnin' about this for years. And you know what? Word got back to them mullahs. Sure. They heard about me. They're afraid of me. And now they're tryin' to get me. It's in the papers. You can look it up. But they ain't got me yet. Because Ah'm a fighter. That's right, Ah'm willin' to fight for mah way of life—mah Christian way of life. When the chips are down, are you?"

Eldon Sluggard took a deep breath. He felt dizzy. He pressed on.

"That's why Eldon Sluggard has decided to take the gloves off. No more speechifyin'. No more warnin'. This is war! These mullahs got a thing they call a *jihad*. You know what that means? It's mullah talk for a holy war. Well, Ah got just the thing to counter their wicked *jihad*. It's called a crusade. You've heard the word, right? But how many of you know what it really means? Well, Ah'll tell you.

"A crusade is a kind of war. But it's not like other wars. This kind of war is blessed by the Almighty. Because regardless of what you may have heard, the Almighty don't want us to turn our cheeks to his enemies. No, God wants us to smite the Moslem heathen. And this is what Ah'm offerin' you. A chance to smite the enemies of Christianity.

"Got your blood worked up, have Ah? Want to know more? Then grab a pencil. There's gonna be a toll-free number coming on at the bottom of your TV screen any second now. Ah want you to write it down. Write it down now. And give me a call. Ah want you to make a pledge for Christ. Ah want you to join my Cross Crusade. No, Ah don't want money. You can keep your money. Ah want you. Yes, you! Ah want you to give me a little of your time. That's all Ah can say on the air. But if you're as worked up as Ah am about these shitty Moslems, you call this minute. There's committed anti-Moslem folks here ready and able to tell you more.

"But before Ah go, Ah want to leave you with this bit of Scripture from Colossians," said Reverend Eldon Sluggard, his voice descending into an attention-getting whisper. " 'For Ah took the flashin' sword of the Lord God and Ah disemboweled my enemies. And yea, with the Lord at my side, Ah clove their heads from their necks, and as the blood spurted, Ah chopped their hands from their wrists, and their feet from their ankles, and when Ah was done, Ah plunged my sword deep into their quiverin' vitals.' "

Eldon Sluggard clapped the big blank book shut.

"And that's how God wants us to deal with his enemies. Won't you join him now and smite a Moslem for Jesus?"

Eldon Sluggard took a deep breath and fixed the camera with a steely stare.

"That's a cut," the director yelled. The red light went out and Eldon Sluggard pulled out a handkerchief and wiped off his sweat-drenched face. He looked under his armpits. They were soaked.

"That was great, El. I've never seen you better."

"Thanks. Have mah media advisers check it over. Then get ready to run it on the commercial spots for today's show. One during the first break and again during the last one."

Eldon Sluggard left the studio. If that didn't get them worked up and calling in by the thousands, nothing would.

It was going to work this time. He could feel it deep inside him.

Three hours later, Eldon Sluggard's *Get with God* program was going out live over the air. After the first fifteen minutes, in which he peddled Eldon Sluggard's

tape-cassette prayers and Eldon Sluggard's five-step plan
to worldly riches, the director cut to the Cross Crusade
commercial.

Eldon Sluggard watched on the monitor. He thought
he had never put more passion in his voice, more fire in
his delivery.

He had excellent reason to. He believed in his Cross
Crusade. It sounded as good today as it did when
Victoria Hoar, her tongue sliding down his belly to the
jackpot, first explained it to him.

"Your ministry is going to hell in a handbasket," she
said.

"Ah know it. Everyone knows it. And Ah'm not alone.
This TV thing has been milked to death."

"Don't talk. Listen."

"You ain't tellin' me anything Ah don't already know.
What Ah want—mmmm. Ahhh . . . oh, God."

When Victoria Hoar's mouth disengaged itself, she
went on speaking. She had Eldon Sluggard's undivided
attention. He was quivering from head to toe.

"The problem is that you've been targeting the same
audience the others have. Everyone has been fishing in
the same pond."

"That's where the big money is. Old ladies. Widows.
The lonely ones. Most of them are on welfare or Social
Security. They got nothing but despair. Ah reach out to
them and Ah say, 'You give me some of that money in
God's name and God will repay you three fold.' They
believe it. Ah call it 'Investing in Heaven.' "

"I call it soaking the gullible."

"It works."

"Did work. But no more."

"Guess it worked too good," Eldon Sluggard mused,
staring at the ceiling.

"The idea is sound. But now you go after the second-
most-gullible demographic group possible."

"Second?"

Victoria Hoar nodded firmly. "Second."

"There's nothing more gullible than a seventy-five-year-old widow with nothing better to do than watch game shows and listen to her joints creak," Reverend Sluggard said flatly.

"Little old ladies don't go off to fight wars."

"Of course not. Who'd be crazy enough to—"

"Teenagers."

"Huh?"

"Specifically teenage boys. Girls seem to mature faster."

"Teenage boys don't have the disposable income. Not to part with. They're all spending it on teenage girls and cars and drugs or whatever. The youth of this nation are going to pot."

"You don't want their money."

"Sure Ah do. Money is what the God Game is all about."

"Not when you can have their bodies," Victoria Hoar said, running her tapered fingers through his pomaded hair.

"Ah don't want their bodies. Ah want *your* body."

"We'll get back to that. But listen. Do you·remember your European history? The Crusades?"

"I didn't go to school much."

"But you know what the Crusades were?"

"Sure, Slim and Jaimie had one before they got all jammed up. They called it their Crusade for Cash. Ah laughed when Ah first heard about it, but the bold approach must have worked. They were raking it in until Jaimie's mascara ran during that press conference rainstorm and everyone saw that she was a he. Gave new meaning to the term TV evangelist."

"That's a different kind of crusade. The original Crusades were launched into the Islamic world by the popes. It was a little like your operation. A scam. They called in soldiers to reclaim Jerusalem in the name of God, but they were really just using God as an excuse to capture land and pillage. It worked for a while, too. They had Jerusalem for a long time."

"What good would that do me? Ah don't want Jerusalem. Hell, the Jews got that sewed up anyway. And they're meaner than snakes when you stick your nose into their patch. Ask any Egyptian."

"I'm not talking about Jerusalem. I'm talking about some of the most coveted land on earth."

"Palm Springs?"

"No. Places like Iran. Iraq. Oil-rich places."

"Oil ain't worth piss these days. Ask any Texan."

"Not now. Not today. Ten years ago, yes. But not now. Do you know why not, El?"

"Too much of it. Market's saturated. Like mine."

"There has always been too much of it. But it's the Iran-Iraq war. While they were fighting they sold cheap to keep their war machines going. Now they're selling cheap to rebuild their shattered economies. OPEC is practically in shambles over it. The price of oil is so soft now that in Houston they can't afford to pump the oil they know is down there. Why bother? The Iranians or Iraqis will only undercut their prices by ten dollars a barrel."

"So?"

"So if someone, some extraordinary person, could gain control over those oil-rich areas, they could dictate the price of oil. And much more."

"How come you know so much about this oil stuff?"

"My daddy's in the oil business."

"And what business are you in?"

"The pleasure business," Victoria Hoar said with a nasty little laugh before she went down on him again.

When Reverend Eldon Sluggard had pried himself off the ceiling, he panted out a question:

"How can Ah make this happen?"

"You have a TV cable network that can reach millions of people. You have a powerful way of speaking. You can do the recruiting. Just shift your efforts to reaching the teenagers of America. They'll respond. Kids these days are very militaristic. Why do you think Vietnam movies are so big? Get them worked up against Iran. Lay it on thick. We'll start a camp here. We'll separate the curious from the committed and then train the committed to fight."

"How do we get them to Iran?"

"I still have connections in the oil business. Leave that part to me. You deliver the crusaders and I'll get them to the crusade."

"Ah don't know. Ah'm tempted. But Iran. It's a big place."

"Seven years of war has drained Iran of fighting men. Its economy is on its back. It's a pariah nation. It can barely hold back the ragtag Mujahideen rebels, and half the populace will see us as liberators. If we can hold the oil fields long enough, the country will fall into anarchy. There will be a mullah hanging from every lamppost. We can just walk in. Trust me."

Reverend Eldon Sluggard considered. Finally he asked, "Can Ah still work the old ladies on the side?"

"All you want," said Victoria Hoar, sitting up and reaching for her neatly folded skirt.

"Hey! What about you?" Eldon Sluggard asked.

"What about me?" Victoria responded, absently hooking her bra.

"I got off twice. You ain't even got off once. Don't you want to?"

"No. I get off making things happen."

They were happening again, thought Eldon Sluggard. The new Cross Crusade spot hadn't even run to the end and the phone banks were lighting up. New recruits were calling at a rate of three a second. Volunteers manning the phones hastily took down the names of the recruits. This time, Eldon Sluggard was going to launch a bigger and better crusade. One that would work. He could feel success now.

Besides, as Victoria Hoar had said just this morning, Eldon Sluggard had no choice. He had angered the mullahs in Tehran. They were after him. And their kind never gave up until they got their way or got run over.

They were not going to get the Reverend Eldon Sluggard, he promised himself. No sirree. Not even if the Pershing Gulf ran red with blood.

13

"You're very good at what you do," Victoria Hoar told the man she knew as Remo Cleaver.

"He is adequate," sniffed Chiun.

"I do all right," Remo said. They were in Eldon Sluggard's conference room. Victoria Hoar was looking into Remo's dark eyes. Remo was looking at her breasts. He decided that his first impression had been wrong. They were not too small. They just looked that way. Probably they were perfectly proportioned for Victoria Hoar's eel-slim body.

"That is what I said," Chiun put in. "He is all right. Another word for 'adequate.' I am glad he admits it."

"Oh, he's just being modest."

"Not him," said Chiun, eyeing the pair with undisguised concern. Victoria Hoar had drifted up to Remo as if he were a flower and she was a bee. Or was it the other way around? Either way, they were drawing together in a pre-copulation way. Chiun knew the signs. He would have to do something about this before Remo ruined their assignment.

"No, not him," Chiun repeated, suddenly appearing in the space between the two. He looked up at Victoria Hoar's dreamy face. "On the other hand, I am modest. Extremely modest. Possibly unsurpassed as a modest person."

But the white woman named Victoria Hoar did not deign to take notice of the Master of Sinanju. She continued looking into Remo's hard face. Chiun looked again. Remo's expression was no longer hard. It was softening. Worse, it was soft.

"Arrggh!" Chiun said.

"What's that you said, Little Father?" Remo asked.

"I said 'Arrggh!' "

"I thought so," Remo said absently.

"Why don't I show you around the grounds?" Victoria Hoar said suddenly, taking Remo by the hand. "Get you acquainted with the fine work of Eldon Sluggard World Ministries."

"A good thought," said Chiun, taking Victoria Hoar by her free hand. "You may show us both around."

Victoria Hoar felt Chiun's hand in hers. It was strong for a hand so frail-looking and thin-boned. She looked down at the shiny head of the tiny Oriental, which was bald but for two white tufts of hair over each ear.

Chiun was smiling up at her. He looked like a pleased little elf. But his hands were grinding the complicated bones of her palm against one another. It hurt. Victoria Hoar attempted to disengage her hand, but the little Oriental would not let go.

"Yes, of course. I did mean both of you," she gasped painfully.

Only then did the pressure stop.

When she led them from the room, Victoria was holding no one's hand.

"What's with her?" Remo whispered as they followed Victoria Hoar down the corridor and into the coolness of the late-spring afternoon.

"Fickle," Chiun said. "I would watch that one."

"Funny. She seemed so warm only a minute ago."

"A certain sign of fickleness," said Chiun. He looked around the quadrangle. "We are obviously working for a man who likes to see his name on everything."

Hearing that, Victoria Hoar turned her head. "Reverend Sluggard believes in glorifying God," she said. She adressed her statement to Remo, not Chiun. Remo smiled. She smiled back. Chiun decided this was an appropriate moment to speak up.

"How does putting his name on every building glorify the Supreme Creator?" he asked.

"Reverend Sluggard is God's representative on earth. What glorifies Reverend Sluggard glorifies God."

"Says who?" asked Chiun.

"Hush, Little Father," Remo admonished. "Victoria is explaining."

"Call me Vicki if you wish," she said, impulsively taking Remo's hand once more. Chiun moved to her other side to grasp the other hand. Obviously this white woman was stubborn. But Chiun saw that she had entwined her arm around Remo's and laid her other hand upon his forearm.

"I asked a question," Chiun said huffily. "Who says this man represents the Supreme Creator?"

"Why, Reverend Sluggard does," said Victoria Hoar, as if that explained everything. "He was fasting one day and God spoke to him. God gave him a holy rapture, and told him to build all this."

"Were there any witnesses?"

"No. Why should there be? God's personal representative would never lie, now, would he?"

"I've been thinking about God a lot lately," Remo said.

As they walked, Victoria pointed out that just last month the Reverend Sluggard had raised over a million dollars, which he donated to the starving people of Ethiopia.

"It used to be two million a month, but donations have dropped off. Those bad religious figures," she added conspiratorially.

"What bad religious figures?" Remo asked.

"Well, there's Slim and Jaimie Barker, Moral Robbins—"

"Never heard of them," said Remo.

"Don't you watch television?" Victoria Hoar wanted to know.

"No, not really," Remo said.

"Or read newspapers?"

"I try to keep up with the Sunday funnies," said Remo.

"Good," said Victoria Hoar.

"How long has this Sluggard been donating money to the starving Ethiopians?" Chiun put in suddenly.

"Oh, I don't know. Years."

"More than two?"

"At least three."

"Then why are the Ethiopians still starving? If you gave them over seventy-two million dollars, even Ethiopians could find a way to feed their populace," said Chiun.

"I don't really know," answered Victoria Hoar. "I never thought about it. I guess they breed faster than we can donate money."

"That makes no sense," Chiun said scornfully.

"Sounds about right to me," Remo said brightly. He was looking into Victoria's eyes again. In another minute, Chiun was sure, they would fall onto the grass and begin rutting in front of everyone. The Master of Sinanju looked around. Maybe if he pretended to stumble against something and break it, the spell would be broken.

There was a towering cross in the middle of the quadrangle. It looked like gold, but Chiun recognized at a glance that it was only brass polished to a high sheen. Etched in the horizontal bar of the cross was a legend, "Do Unto Others . . ."

"Why is the rest of the quotation missing?" Chiun asked suddenly. He had decided against destroying the cross. Knowing Remo's present sensitivity, he would probably accuse the Master of Sinanju of violating some silly white taboo.

"What?" asked Victoria Hoar, whirling. Her eyes

followed Chiun's pointing finger to the cross. "Oh, that. I think they couldn't fit it all in."

"There is plenty of room," said Chiun.

"Reverend Sluggard says it's easier to remember."

"It changes the meaning," said Chiun.

"Is he always like that?" Victoria asked Remo.

Remo nodded. "And this is one of his good days."

"I heard that," snapped Chiun. He hurried to catch up with them. The female was leading Remo to a building marked "World Broadcast Ministries." Chiun understood that had something to do with television. Perhaps this female wanted to copulate with Remo in front of a TV camera for all the world to see. The Master of Sinanju had heard that there were harlots in America who did such things for money. He decided that they were in an evil place and the sooner they were done with this assignment, the better.

Naturally, it was at that moment that Remo chose to say what was on his mind.

"You know, I kind of like it here. It reminds me of when I used to go to Sunday school. The crosses. The cool breezes on the grass. Everything is so clean and pure. I was thinking just the other day that it's been years since I've been to church. Wasn't I, Chiun?"

"I am not privy to your ridiculous thoughts," Chiun grumbled. "Except when you insist on braying them to anyone who will listen."

"A lot of people find inner peace through Reverend Sluggard," Victoria said musically. "He was telling me just the other day that he's had wonderful success with teenage boys. I guess they're drawn to him because he's so filled with the Holy Spirit."

"I guess everyone here prays a lot."

"Are you kidding?" Victoria said dryly. "Reverend Sluggard has me get down on my knees two or three times a day."

"I'd like to hear him preach," Remo said.

"He is a magnificent preacher. Why, he knows the

entire Bible by heart. He can open it up to any page, and without glancing at the page more than a second, recite entire passages."

"I knew a nun who could do that. Sister Mary Margaret," Remo said in a wistful voice. "She was a big influence on my life."

"But at the first sign of disappointment, she spurned you," Chiun put in. Remo ignored him.

"Where are those people going?" asked Remo. He pointed to a dome-shaped glass building. Buses were pulling up in front of it.

"That's the Temple of Tribute," Victoria Hoar said. "It's where Reverend Sluggard pays tribute to the Lord and his flock pays tribute to Reverend Sluggard. Each day, after he tapes his daily program, Reverend Sluggard ministers to the faithful. These people come from all over the country to receive Reverend Sluggard's blessing. He heals through faith. I have an idea. Why don't we watch him work? We can finish the tour later."

"Is that all right with you, Little Father?" Remo asked suddenly. "I really want to see this."

The Master of Sinanju hesitated. He would have said no, but Remo had asked, and there was another reason.

"Yes, let us all go," Chiun said. "I am curious to see how American religions work. Perhaps I can learn how they so enthrall even those who have been raised above them."

They melted into the converging groups. The Master of Sinanju noticed that most of the people were old. Many had infirmities. Some walked on crutches. Others were pushed along in wheelchairs. Many joints made tiny sounds of misalignment. Here and there, hearts beat irregularly. Heart disease. It was common in America, he knew. In his home village of Sinanju on the West Korea Bay, it was nearly unheard-of, thanks to a steady diet of fish and rice.

The interior of the Temple of Tribute was a great

circular room. The roof was like the inside of a crystal cone. Beams of white pine supported it, and shafts of radiant sunlight kissed the seat sections, which resembled a pie cut into four wedges. And in the center, there sat a raised dais and a podium with a microphone. Every element was either glass or white pine or birchwood.

"Let's sit up front," said Victoria Hoar, leading Remo by the hand. She had to push through the crowd to get to the first row. When she arrived, she blinked.

The Master of Sinanju, who had been behind them, was already seated.

"I saved seats for both of you," he said, beaming. He indicated a seat on his left for Victoria and a seat on his right for Remo. All the other first-row seats were occupied.

Victoria took her seat, fuming. Remo was sniffing the air.

"Incense," he said.

"Sandalwood. A terrible kind," Chiun said, wrinkling his nose.

"I don't know. It kinda reminds me of the incense they used to burn in Saint Andrews. Makes me feel kinda nostalgic."

"Is that another word for 'nauseated'?" asked Chiun.

When the room had filled, there was a long pause. Organ music came in through the loudspeakers. And from behind a door curtained in white strode the Reverend Eldon Sluggard. His meaty frame was encased in a white silk suit accented by a canary-yellow tie. He stepped up to the podium to thunderous applause.

Chiun watched carefully. Never had he heard of a priest who was greeted by his faithful followers with applause. Was this some new wrinkle the American whites had added to Christianity? Perhaps there was something to be learned here after all.

"You!" shouted Reverend Eldon Sluggard. The word bounced off the accoustically perfect ceiling panes. The applause stopped dead. The echoes of the word hung in the sandalwood-laden air.

"You! You! And you! You are all sinners before God," yelled Reverend Eldon Sluggard, stabbing a fat finger at the audience.

"You are the dust beneath the feet of the truly righteous.

"You are the dirt that is consumed by the lowly worm.

"You are scum, all of you. All of you!" Reverend Eldon Sluggard's holy righteous voice resounded through the Temple of Tribute.

"Obviously he means those other than his security force," the Master of Sinanju whispered to Remo.

"Hush!" said Remo. "I want to hear this."

"All of you!" shouted Eldon Sluggard. His eyes scourged the first row.

The Master of Sinanju jumped to his feet. "Did you hear that, Remo? He has insulted my awesome personage. For that I will—"

Remo flashed to his feet. "Sit down! You want to ruin everything?"

"But he has insulted me."

"It's just his style. They call it fire and brimstone. It's traditional."

"I call it base and insulting," said Chiun.

"Please!"

Reluctantly the Master of Sinanju returned to his seat. Reverend Eldon Sluggard continued speaking, his head held high, his voice reverberating. He had not noticed Chiun's outburst.

"You are the maggots in the roadside garbage," Reverend Sluggard went on. "Ah know that. You know it. Admit it. Don't be ashamed. Say it with me, 'Ah am a maggot.' "

"I am a maggot," chorused the crowd.

The Master of Sinanju turned around. A sea of wrinkled, ailing faces held rapt expressions. Their mouths repeated the insane insults of the Reverend Eldon Sluggard.

"That's the bad news," said Reverend Sluggard. "But the good news is that you're no ordinary maggots. No! You're God's maggots."

"Hallelujah!" returned the crowd.

The Master of Sinanju blinked. What manner of madness was this?

"The Lord's holy maggots," howled Reverend Sluggard. "You may be squirmin' in the garbage now, but come Judgment Day, you're a-gonna sprout wings and fly."

"Praise be!"

"But God ain't gonna give you them wings until you've proved your love for him. Until you give tribute to him. Now, Ah know you're in need. Only the needy come to me. Can't pay those bills? Tell you what you do. Instead of scrimpin' a few more weeks to get enough money to pay the rent, give me that money. That's right! Give it to the Reverend Sluggard. Ah'm gonna invest it for you. And what am Ah gonna invest it in? Not in the stock market. Not in CD's. No, Ah'm gonna invest it in God. And God is gonna pay you back, yes sirree. You know that even if you scrape up your rent money, it's only gonna come due next month and you're gonna have to scrimp and save and pinch pennies all over again. But if you have faith, God's gonna give you a return on your investment. And Ah don't mean ten percent. No, Ah mean a thousand percent. You'll never have to scrimp and save again."

"Glory!"

"Now, maybe some of you say, 'Reverend Sluggard, my problem's got nothin' to do with money. Well, good for you, Ah say. Maybe it's health. Maybe you got a bad back or lumbago, or dropsy, or some such ailment. Well, you know that ain't your fault, any more than bein' poor is. It's the work of Satan! Admit it!"

"Amen!"

"Satan's put a curse on you! He's sapped your strength. He's poisoned your blood. Well, Ah got a cure for that too. And it's called faith. What's that, you say? Ah can hear your thoughts. The Lord lets me see into your minds, Ah'm so full of the Holy Spirit tonight. You say you don't have enough faith? Well, you don't have to. Because Ah got the faith. Yea, let mah faith show you the way. Now, later on Ah'm gonna come among you and start layin' hands on some of you. Do you have cancer? Ah'm gonna cure you. Do you have emphysema? Well, get ready to breathe free again!"

"This is the thrilling part," Victoria whispered.

"I've heard of faith healing," said Remo.

"And I have heard of charlatanry," snapped Chiun.

"But first," said Reverend Sluggard, "my acolytes are gonna come among you. They have envelopes. You know what they're for. They have credit-card slips and those little *ka-chunka* charge machines. Don't worry if you don't know how to work them. That's what my acolytes are here for."

Out of the curtained door came a handful of men and women in white garments. The men wore white suits with white shoes and ties. The women were in demure white dresses. The way the men dressed reminded Remo of his First Communion suit.

They went among the crowd. The women passed out the envelopes at one end of each wedge of seats. The men collected them after they were passed, crammed full of cash, to the other ends. Those who chose to pay by credit card were invited into the aisles, where little folding tables were set up. Credit-card machines went *chunka-thunk* so regularly, it was as if a million engines were at work at some relentless task.

Chiun's narrow eyes widened. Tribute. This priest was exacting tribute from his followers. He wondered what Remo had to say about this. But when he looked, Remo was watching the Reverend Eldon Sluggard with fascinated eyes.

The Reverend Sluggard was reading from the Bible.

"Let me share with you this verse from Last Corinthians," he was saying. " 'He who shares his bounty with me, no matter how poor, will receive my blessin'. He who gives his last shekel to mah followers will receive plenty in return.' Amen."

"Amazing," said Remo. "He only glanced at that page. He must know the entire book by heart."

"Why not?" said Chiun. "He knows every other trick in the book."

"What's that, Little Father?" Remo asked, turning.

"Never mind. I do not converse with the deaf and blind."

When the collection of money stopped, Reverend Sluggard descended from the podium.

"Those wishin' healin', form two lines before me," Reverend Sluggard announced, raising up his many-ringed hands.

Before the words were out of his mouth, there was a surge to the aisle he stood in. Remo saw old women bent nearly double. Men in wheelchairs. People whose eye whites were greenish from diseases of the blood and organs.

A man was being helped by relatives to stand before Reverend Sluggard. His left foot was encased in bandages. He had to hop to reach the spot, his arms resting on the shoulders of two others.

"And what is your ailment, brother?" asked Reverend Sluggard.

"I got gout," the man croaked.

"Gout!" said Reverend Sluggard.

"I can't walk on my left foot. It hurts something fierce. Has for over three years now."

"You know what gout is, brother?" said Reverend Sluggard for all to hear.

"Yes."

"It's another word for Satan. I'll bet the doctor told you he can't cure you."

"That's right, Reverend."

"And you know what? He was right."

Tears of disappointment appeared in the corners of the old man's eyes.

"He can't. But Ah can. And the reason Ah can is that Ah know you can't get rid of the devil with pills or medicines. You get rid of Satan by castin' him out. And you all watch. Ah'm gonna cast out that old devil called gout."

And placing his hands on the man's thining hair, Reverend Eldon Sluggard raised his voice to the rafters. "Powers of Satan, Ah command you to be gone. Leave this poor old man be. Spirits of Darkness, Ah cast you out!"

The old man winced with each shouted word.

"Now," said Reverend Sluggard, stepping back. "Ah say to you, brother, stand free from Satan's shackles. You, on either side, let him go. He don't need your support no more."

The supporting pair let go of the man.

Without support, he was forced to put his weight on his heavily bandaged foot.

"Now, walk toward me."

"I . . . I'm afraid."

"Come on, come on. Ah got enough faith for both of us. Walk!"

The old man took a hobbling step. His feet supported him.

"Look," he shouted. "Look, I'm healed. I can *walk!*"

"*Hallelujah!*"

"Sure you can walk." Reverend Sluggard grinned. "The devil's been cast out of your foot. Now you know what you gotta do next?"

"Pray!" said the old man.

"No. You go right over to that nice girl in white and you show God how thankful you are. You go and double your contribution."

The old man went obligingly. His step was firm.

"Amazing," said Remo.

"This will go on all day," said Victoria.

"Pah!" spat Chiun in a disgusted voice. He watched the old man walk over to the girl and hand her more money. Then the man went back to his seat. By the time he got to his aisle, Chiun noticed that he was beginning to favor his bandaged foot again.

But no one else noticed. Their eyes were on Reverend Eldon Sluggard. He was curing a little girl of pancreatic cancer. The little girl said she felt better when Reverend Sluggard told her she was cured. Her mother wept for joy. A man with cirrhosis of the liver was next. Reverend Sluggard laid his hand upon the man's abdomen and shouted to the rafters. He pronounced the man cured.

The Master of Sinanju noticed a blind man in one of the lines. He was alone. He was asking to be brought before the Reverend Eldon Sluggard. He wanted to see again. His voice was pleading. Only Chiun noticed him.

Then two of the white-clad acolytes discovered the man and took him by the arms. Quietly but firmly they led him out of line and out of the Temple of Tribute. Even over Reverend Sluggard's shoutings, Chiun heard them promise that they were taking him to Reverend Sluggard, who would cure his vision.

An hour later, when the last person threw away his crutches, the blind man had not returned. Chiun knew why. You could convince anyone he was cured of an inner ailment, or that his feeble limbs were empowered once again—at least as long as his euphoria was maintained—but no one could convince a blind man that he could see color and shape.

Chiun frowned as he left the Temple of Tribute. Was this what passed for faith in America? he wondered. Was this the faith that Remo clung to despite having had his vision cleared by Sinanju, his senses made whole?

Remo and Victoria joined the Master of Sinanju in the quadrangle. The congregation was returning to the buses. Chiun noticed that one of the persons who had left their wheelchairs behind had to be helped into the waiting bus.

"Wasn't that inspiring?" Victoria said, squeezing Remo's arm.

"You know how I feel?" Remo said. "I feel exactly the way I used to feel when I would come out of confession."

"Stupid?" asked Chiun.

"No. Sort of . . . purged."

"Ah. I know that feeling," Chiun remarked.

"You do? I didn't know they had anything like confession in Sinanju."

"We do not. We have something equally efficacious."

"Yeah? What's that?"

"Chamber pots."

14

The Master of Sinanju wore his concern on his gracious face.

Not that anyone cared. Especially Remo.

A week had passed. Remo was standing in the wings of the studio where Reverend Eldon Sluggard was taping the latest edition of his *Get with God* program. Chiun did not understand the meaning of the name and had asked Remo to explain it.

"It's slang," Remo had replied. "It means . . . to be one with God. These people in the studio audience want to be one with the Lord."

"They wish to die?"

"No, of course not."

"I am confused. Is it not said in Western religions that in order to be one with the Supreme Creator, death must first occur?"

"Well, yes. But some people believe that it's possible to know God spiritually."

"How?"

"I don't know how it works. But the nuns used to talk about it all the time."

"Ah," said Chiun, "the nuns. And you believed them, although they offered no proof to you?"

"This is faith, Chiun. You don't need proof. You need faith."

"In what?"

"In God."

"Have you ever spoken to this being you call God?"

"No. But the nuns told me all about him. Just like Reverend Sluggard is doing now."

"Do you have faith in Reverend Sluggard?"

"Sure," Remo said quickly.

"And why?"

"Because he's the leader of an important movement. He does good for people. He shows them the way to become the best they can be. Everyone says so."

"And if everyone told you he was a false prophet, would you believe that as well?"

"If he's not the man of God everyone says, why would the Iranians single him out for attack? Answer that."

"And that is your proof of this man's holiness?"

"What else could it mean?" Remo demanded.

"It could be that he angered them."

"Sure he has. He's been warning us about the Moslem threat for years. He told me so. Besides, why would Smith send us to protect him? Huh?"

"I see your newfound faith extends also to Smith," Chiun said quietly. "It is unfortunate." And while Remo's attention remained on the Reverend Sluggard, the Master of Sinanju departed in silence. He repaired to the quarters that had been set aside for them. The quarters were in the great boat that Eldon Sluggard used for his living place. It was explained that Remo and Chiun had to stay close to Reverend Sluggard at all times to protect him from the godless Moslems.

Chiun had replied that the Moslems were not godless. Otherwise they would not be Moslems. Victoria Hoar had countered that Moslems believed in the wrong God.

Chiun had started to ask her how she knew there was a right God, when he realized the stupidity of his own question. There was only one Supreme Creator. Only the name by which different peoples addressed him differed. And over that, non-Koreans had made war throughout history.

Chiun entered his stateroom and went to the telephone device. Ordinarily he despised the machines. They always rang when he was watching something particularly enlightened, and the calls were usually for Remo. Normally, Remo handled all telephonic work, but this was one conversation that the Master of Sinanju did not want Remo to be privy to.

Chiun picked up the receiver and pressed O for Operator. The operator came on the line and Chiun said, "I wish to speak with Harold Smith."

"What city, please?" the operator asked politely.

"It is the city named after one of your breads."

"Bread?"

"Yes, in the province of New York."

"City or state?"

"Is there a difference?" demanded the Master of Sinanju impatiently. "It is the one where Harold Smith resides." Why was it that these whites insisted on giving the same name to entirely different places? Usually names stolen from other countries. Once he had noticed a Cairo, Illinois, and a Carthage, New York, on a map. There were also a Paris, Texas, and a Troy, Ohio. Chiun once awoke from a particularly terrible nightmare in which the mothers of his village were forced to once again drown their starving babies as they did in the old times, because ignorant modern kings had been sending their emissaries to negotiate with the Master of Sinanju, Utah.

"New York City is in New York State," said the operator.

"Then it is in New York State because New York City is south of this place, which is called Folcroft."

"I don't have a listing for a Folcroft, New York," said the operator.

"I did not say the town was called Folcroft, stupid woman," Chiun snapped. "I said it was one of your bread names. Folcroft is the building."

"There is no need to shout, sir," the operator said indignantly.

"I am waiting."

"I have a listing for a Folcroft Sanitarium in Rye, New York. Is that what you want?"

"Of course. What other Folcrofts are there? Never mind," Chiun said quickly, realizing that he might have to listen to a twelve-hour recitation of all the other American Folcrofts. "I wish to speak with Harold Smith."

"And your name?"

"I am under cover and forbidden to identify myself."

"Er, one moment."

After a few seconds, a telephone ringing greeted Chiun's eager ears. The dry voice of Dr. Harold W. Smith, known in the Book of Sinanju variously as Smith the First, Smith the Generous, Smith the Frugal, and Mad Harold, said, "Hello?"

"I have a collect call for Harold Smith."

"From whom?" Smith asked suspiciously.

"The gentleman refuses to identify himself."

"I do not accept collect calls from strangers," Smith snapped.

"It is not strangers, it is I," said Chiun suddenly.

"Please, sir," the operator said. "You are not permitted to talk to the other party unless he agrees to accept the call."

"I will accept," Smith said quickly. "Go ahead, Master of . . . er, Master."

The operator got off the line and Chiun launched into his complaint.

"Emperor Smith, we have a problem."

"Yes?" Smith's voice was tight.

"It is Remo. I fear he will be unable to accomplish this assignment."

"Is he injured?"

"Yes, mentally injured. He is suffering greatly. He talks of incense and vestal virgins he knew in his earlier life, and there is a new woman who has him in her thrall."

"I'm afraid Remo's romantic predilections are not sufficient to pull him off this assignment."

"He is being poisoned by this place. I fear that if he remains any longer, he will go over to the enemy."

"What enemy?"

"Reverend Sluggard."

"I have no information indicating that Sluggard is anything but a target of Iranian fundamentalists. What makes you say he is the enemy?"

"Anyone who speaks honeyed words that draw Remo away from the path of Sinanju is the enemy."

"I see. Are you saying that Remo is experiencing a religious conversion of some type?"

"I would not call it that. I would call it a reversion. It is all he talks about now. Faith and sin and other trivia."

"I'm sorry, Master Chiun. I agree with you that if Remo is experiencing a religious reawakening, that could cause problems for us, but right now this assignment must be carried out. Have you learned anything?"

"Yes. It was during this priest's television program. He is launching a Crusade."

"So?"

"A Crusade," repeated Chiun. "Do you not know your history?"

"Of course I do," Smith said peevishly, the insult in his voice for once matching Chiun's. He was proud of his straight-A pluses in history that started in the fifth grade and continued, an unbroken testament to Smith's studiousness and lack of a normal social life, all the way up to his graduation from Dartmouth College.

"Are you not concerned?"

"I think you misunderstand," said Smith reasonably. "Sluggard is not talking about a crusade in the sense of the old incursions into the Holy Land, but a crusade for funds."

"I have seen how he tricks people out of money, too. But I heard the words he spoke. He spoke of a holy war."

"Many of these television ministers solicit money in different ways. And regardless of how questionable Sluggard's methods may be, our concern is not that, but in any activities that might have attracted the attention of the Iranian hierarchy."

"Then send Remo and me to Iran. We are known there. We will talk to their caliph. We will find your answers, and negotiate an excellent treaty. But in this place, we will learn nothing and perhaps lose our Remo."

"I'm sorry, master Chiun. Relations with the Iranians are very sensitive at this moment. We can't be seen doing business with them and we don't dare stir them up any more than they have been. Do your best at this end. Good-bye."

The Master of Sinanju slammed down the receiver. Of course it cracked. Why did they insist upon making these aggravating instruments out of plastic and not iron? Iron did not shatter under normal use.

At his Folcroft office, Dr. Harold W. Smith frowned as he returned to his computer. He was worried about the situation. It was unusual for Chiun to contact him. No doubt his concern for Remo was well-intentioned, even well-placed, but time was of the essence.

Already Smith was reading the signs of a new wave of terrorist activities.

In Boston a private security agency whose uniformed employees were composed of Lebanese engineering students was showing a sudden surge of activity having nothing to do with its billable clients. Smith alerted the Boston branch of the FBI.

In Beirut, members of the Iranian-backed Hezbollah militia were filtering out of the city to transit points, presumably bound for the West. Smith alerted U.S. immigration.

And in Iran, the Iranian Parliament was calling for severe punishment against U.S. aggressions. Iran was always calling for the U.S. to be punished for imagined aggressions. It was a day-to-day activity designed to keep their Revolution alive. Smith called up the details. It was usually the same. Imaginary nonsense promulgated for domestic consumption.

What Smith found was the usual hysteria and threats. Iran claimed a U.S. invasion force had attempted to enter the country. They claimed as proof a number of bodies of American mercenaries, and they had taken hostage a U.S. oil tanker, the *Seawise Behemoth*, which had been used to smuggle in the invading force. Smith's computers informed him that there were no traceable links between the oil company that owned the tanker and Sluggard's organization.

There were daily demonstrations in the streets of Tehran in which the alleged instigator of the attack, Reverend Eldon Sluggard, was burned in effigy on a wooden cross.

Smith almost laughed aloud. The idea of a television preacher launching a military strike into the Middle East in cooperation with an oil company was too bizarre even for Iranian propaganda.

One item showing up on his computer search did get Harold Smith's attention.

A Sapulpa, Oklahoma, couple, Don and Bessie Booe, was filing a suit against the Reverend Eldon Sluggard. They claimed that their son, Lamar, had gone on a retreat to Sluggard's Christian Campground and disappeared.

According to Sluggard's people, Lamar Booe had left the retreat after only a week, citing his lack of faith. The Booes countered that claim by producing letters from their son, purportedly written more than a month after Sluggard's people claimed he had left the Christian Campground, as proof of their story.

Although it seemed to be merely a case of a young

man who perhaps couldn't face his parents after failing
to live up to their expectations, Smith called up all
available data from the news-media file. At this point,
anything unusual pertaining to Reverend Eldon Sluggard and his ministry could not be overlooked, no matter how inconsequential.

15

The red light winked out and Reverend Eldon Sluggard collapsed into a plush chair. The overhead spotlights were killing him. The cameramen began pulling their now-inactive equipment away from the set.

"El, I have to tell you," the director said effusively, "that was your best show ever. You were positively inspired."

"Thanks," said the Reverend Eldon Sluggard as he wiped the sheen of sweat from his brow. After changing handkerchiefs twice, he saw that the cloth was still coming away sopping. He was thinking that for once he wasn't positively inspired. He was negatively inspired. If he didn't pull in enough recruits to make a difference, his head was going to end up on a post in Persia—or whatever it was called now. "Now, do me a favor? Clear out all these technical people and get me Victoria Hoar."

"Check."

While Reverend Sluggard waited, someone came up behind him.

"I just wanted to tell you," a voice said while Reverend Sluggard jumped a foot into the air with fright, "what an inspiring sermon that was."

"Whoee! Don't you sneak up on me like that again!" said the Reverend Sluggard when he recognized his bodyguard.

"Sorry!" Remo said in a sheepish voice.

" 'S all right. Ah get really wound up after one of these things."

"I was wondering if you could explain something to me."

"What's that?"

"You were talking about repentance earlier. When I was a kid, we'd go to confession, the priest blessed us, and we had to say a few 'Hail Marys,' a couple of 'Our Fathers,' and an 'Act of Contrition.' But how does it work here?"

"Got sins hanging heavy on your soul?"

"Well," Remo admitted, "it's been a while."

"Do you feel sorry for them, son?" asked Reverend Sluggard, his voice sinking into an oily unctuousness.

"Yeah."

"And you want the good Lord to forgive you?"

"Do you think he would?"

"How much money you got on you?"

"Money?" Remo said vaguely. He dug into his wallet. "I don't know," he said as he started to count out the contents. "Maybe—"

"That's enough," said Eldon Sluggard, snatching the money away. "You're forgiven."

"I am?" Remo asked blankly.

"Ah said so, didn't Ah?"

"But it doesn't seem . . . I mean it . . ."

"Son, when you used to tell the priest about how sinful you were, how long did it take you to go right on doing what you were ashamed to tell the priest you were doing in the first place?"

"Oh, a couple of days. A week at most."

"And you know why?"

"No."

"Because all the priest asked of you was to say a few prayers. Prayers are easy, son. Prayers are cheap. Any sinner can pray. But money, that's different. Do you for one godly minute think that if every sinner had to fork over his grocery money when he confessed to sin, he'd be so quick to keep right on sinnin'?"

"No. . . ." Remo said slowly.

"No! That's right! No, he would not. He'd waver. He'd think twice, and then thrice. Because money is substantial. Money is important. Everyone knows it. Don't you think God knows it too? That's why he sent you here."

"Actually, it was someone else's idea," Remo put in.

"Someone who was inspired by the Holy Spirit!"

Remo's brow gathered in thought. He tried to imagine Dr. Harold W. Smith motivated by the Holy Spirit. The image wouldn't come. Maybe he wasn't imagining hard enough.

"The Holy Spirit brought you here. And you know why?" Before Remo could open his mouth, Reverend Eldon Sluggard answered his own question. "Because he knew you needed saving and that the starving people of Ethiopia needed this money. This is God's money now. It's gonna be put to good use. And so are you. Tell you what. Ah'm gonna confer with one of mah advisers about how best to get this money to Ethiopia. Why don't you check on security?"

"I had another question," Remo started to say.

"Time enough for that later. Now, off with you. We gotta keep this house of the Lord inviolate from the heathen."

Reluctantly Remo left the studio. Reverend Eldon Sluggard watched him go.

"That boy may be fast with his hands," Reverend Eldon Sluggard muttered, "but he won't win no contests for mental brilliance."

When Victoria Hoar found Reverend Sluggard, he was counting Remo's money.

"How are the new security people working out?" she asked.

"Ah may not have to pay the tall one. He fell for the

old cash-for-forgiveness hustle. But that ain't why Ah called you. We got another problem."

"What's that?"

"My legal staff says we're being sued. Over one of those recruits. His parents say they ain't heard from him."

"I thought you had your staff writing letters home for all of them to cover their disappearance."

"Ah did. This is the one what went pacifist on me during the last phase of training. He had seen too much, so we convinced him that if he carried the banner of the Crusade, he wouldn't have to carry a weapon. but Ah guess he wrote home that he was quittin' before we got his mind turned around. Now his folks are yellin' and carryin' on that their son has been kidnapped or some fool thing."

"This could get serious when the relatives of the other recruits hear of this."

"Ah hadn't counted on them all dyin'," Reverend Eldon Sluggard complained. "What was wrong with them? They had the best weapons money could buy. The best trainin'. And most of all, they had motivation. They should have torn through them ragheads like a pack of buzz saws."

"The next Crusade will have to be better-trained and better-equipped."

"And better-motivated," added Reverend Sluggard. "It's mah sacred ass."

"I have an idea how to do that."

"Yeah? Lemme hear."

"At a more opportune time. We have better things to do."

"Amen. While we're alone," Reverend Sluggard suggested, breaking out into a Cheshire grin, "how about a little unholy communion?"

"Not now. I want to check on the new security people. They could be a problem."

"Ah noticed you been eyeing the tall one."

"Of course. If he's drooling over me, he won't see the obvious."

"Good point. But one thing Ah still ain't figured out: who are they? How can they do all that weird stuff they do?"

"I don't know. But I think the technique they used on the old security chief was created by the ninjas."

"Which sect are they? Ah don't pay too much attention to cults."

"The ninjas were Japanese espionage agents. They possessed remarkable stealth and killing tactics."

"That would make the old man a Japanese. But not the white one. He ain't no more Japanese than my daddy."

"Who knows? But I'll find out. As long as Remo believes in your ministry, and my smile, we can control him."

"Amen, sister."

16

Rashid Shiraz had no problem with Customs at Montreal International Airport. His passport was in order. It identified him as Barsoom Basti, a Turk. No one from Lebanon to Ankara would mistake Rashid for a Turk, but in the West they clumped all dusky-skinned people into one racial lump they called Arabs. The guard stamped his passport automatically.

This was the crucial moment. He had gone first, in case the American made a mess of it. He could still run. And in Montreal, which was fast becoming the Vienna of the modern espionage world, there were many people and many places that would provide Rashid Shiraz with safe haven.

Lamar Booe offered his passport. It too was false. It identified him as an Englishman. If Lamar spoke softly, his twangy American accent would not betray him.

Lamar answered the questions in a dull monosyllabic tone and Rashid nodded. It was working. The man was so broken that he would do whatever Rashid asked— even without prompting.

The passport was stamped with a bang and Lamar joined Rashid. They walked from the airport and took a cab to a certain hotel. Within an hour, two Iranians were knocking at the door.

"Is this the dog?" asked one in a hard voice.

"Yes. Pitiful, is he not?"

"Yes," said the Iranian. He turned his attention back to Rashid. "We have a car waiting for you. Driving across the border will be easy. The guards look for drugs and contraband. Be certain you have no weapons with you. You will pass easily. The others are grouping at the rendezvous point."

"You have a map to the place of this false *kafif* Sluggard?"

"*Ari*. Here. And American money. More than you will need. Also there is a picture. You will need it if you are to locate him personally. He often moves with an entourage."

"I may not need it," said Rashid Shiraz.

"Your task is to abduct him and bring him to us. If this is impossible, you may kill him so long as you do it painfully."

"I know this. But this one will see that I am brought before Sluggard."

"How do you know he will not betray you?"

"Because he hates Sluggard more than we do," said Rashid Shiraz. And to prove his point, he extracted the photograph of the Reverend Eldon Sluggard from the folder and, after glancing at it briefly, placed it in Lamar Booe's empty, trembling hands.

"Is this the devil who betrayed you?" Rashid demanded.

"Aaahh!" said Lamar Booe, squeezing the photograph into a crumpled shape. Then, making little mewling sounds of pain, he tore the photograph first into big pieces, then into small pieces. He stopped only when the remaining pieces were so small his fingers could not grip them for further destruction.

His lips moved. The words were barely audible. Lamar Booe was whispering *"Marg bar Sluggard"* over and over in poor Farsi.

17

Remo put his head in through the half-open door.

"Have you seen Victoria?" he asked.

"Too often," Chiun replied sourly.

"The same to you. If you do see her, tell her I'm looking for her."

"Why?" asked Chiun. He was seated on a tatami mat in his stateroom aboard the Reverend Eldon Sluggard's yacht, the *Mary Magdalene*. He was boiling water in a brass bowl suspended over a tiny wood stove. It was his personal rice-making set, used when the Master was not in civilization. It had arrived within the green-gold lacquered trunk only a few hours ago, shipped by Harold Smith from Folcroft Sanitarium to a series of relay points and finally to the Eldon Sluggard World Ministries.

"Because I asked you," Remo said quietly. His tone was not peevish, nor was it demanding. It was, if anything, troubled.

"That is not the why," said Chiun, spooning brown rice grains out of a glazed celadon container in the shape of a bear. "The why is why do you want to see her? Not the other why."

"Because I do."

"I see. And has it anything to do with the troubled tone I detect in your voice?"

"How do you know I'm troubled?"

"Because you are. It is self-evident."

"Yeah?" Remo shifted on his feet. "Well, I thought she could explain something to me."

Chiun turned suddenly, a wooden ladle of rice poised over the happily bubbling water.

"Oh? Do you think that woman can explain what troubles you better than I?"

Remo hesitated. "Yeah, I guess. Probably. It's about Reverend Sluggard. And she's his personal adviser, after all."

"I can tell you all you need to know about this priest."

Remo was half in and half out of the door. He thought a moment and entered the stateroom, closing the door behind him. Chiun pretended to examine the boiling rice closely so that Remo did not behold the slight tug of satisfaction pulling at his lips. He let the final grains of rice mix with the others.

"I am having rice. Will you have some?"

"I'm not hungry," Remo said, joining him on the floor.

Listening to Remo's voice, Chiun added two more ladles full. Enough for Remo.

"So," Chiun said, lifting his face. "What is it that troubles you now?"

"I just had a talk with Reverend Sluggard. I asked him about receiving forgiveness for my sins."

"Ah. That."

"And you know what he did? He took all my money and said I was forgiven."

"Why does that surprise you, Remo? Reverend Sluggard takes everyone's money. For a holy man, he acts like the hated tax collectors the Romans once set upon the Jews and the Christians."

"He puts it to good use. You saw all the people he healed."

"Pah! An old game. A conjurer shouts loudly, causing the heart to beat faster, the pulse to quicken, the mind to concentrate. Or he speaks soothing words that inspire belief in the self. Or he does both. I have seen it many times in many lands. Sluggard does both. And fools believe that they are healed."

"I saw lame people walk. Others get up from wheelchairs."

"I saw the same. The truth is, those people healed themselves."

"What's the difference? They're healed, aren't they?"

"The difference is that their healing will last only as long as their hearts beat fast and their minds are filled with that belief. I saw some of them falter as they returned to their seats. No one else was watching because their minds were on the healer, not the healed."

"If you say you saw it, you saw it," Remo muttered defensively.

"So speaks Remo Williams, the stubborn."

"When Reverend Sluggard told me that God forgave my sins because I gave him all my money, it made sense. It even reminded me of some of your lessons."

"Mine? How so?"

"I don't know. It was the way he explained it, I guess. It started off as one thing and ended up as another. The point he made was that if I was simply forgiven, I wouldn't learn. But if I paid a price, I would learn not to commit the same sins again."

"That is sound reasoning. So why are you troubled? You have paid your tax to this man and he has promised you a blessing in return. What could be more equitable?"

"Well, I don't feel the same way as when I was a kid leaving confession. You know, cleansed."

"Ah, then you question this man?"

"Not exactly. This isn't the Catholic way. It's different. Maybe I'm not supposed to feel the same way as I did then."

"I think there may be enough rice for you," said Chiun, tending to the boiling pot. "If I take less, that is."

"No, thanks," said Remo, shaking his head.

"Do you remember the first time I taught you to overcome heights?"

Remo considered. "I remember the first time you tried."

"That is it."

Remo's face clouded over. "You took me out into these woods where you had miles of logs laid end to end. You made me put on a blindfold and pretend the logs were over a ravine. I climbed on and started walking."

"It was not hard."

"No, not until you told me to take off the blindfold and I found myself standing on a log that was suspended between two cliffs."

"You did not fall."

"I could have!"

"You did not fall when you walked along the first twenty logs. Why would you fall from the twenty-first, just because it was not as close to the ground as you imagined it to be?"

"That's not the point. I could have."

"The point is that you did not."

"So what's the point of reliving it now?" demanded Remo. The old anger was rising in his voice. Chiun found it reassuring, although disrespectful.

"Do you remember, only weeks later, when I again asked you to do something for me?"

"No."

"I asked you to run through a burning room."

"Yeah. It's coming back. You opened the door and there were flames coming from different spots on the floor. Little flames. Tiny ones."

"And I told you to run as if the entire room was ablaze. To run with your eyes shut and your breath held tightly within you."

"And when I was halfway through the little fires, the room exploded in a ball of hell. Christ, Chiun, how could you?"

Chiun shrugged. "A simple mechanical contrivance. The floor contained gas jets. Smith installed them when I insisted that he build me a room for that purpose. I merely turned a wheel."

"I could have been incinerated," Remo growled.

"But you were not. And so you learned that flame is no more to be feared than water if you keep moving and do not inhale. But that is not the point of this discussion either."

"And just what is the friggin' point?" Remo snarled.

"The point is that even though I had tricked you with the logs, you trusted me with the room of fire."

"I was stupid. Sue me."

"Most stupid," Chiun corrected. "Gullible."

"Okay, gullible."

"Hopelessly gullible. Magnificently gullible. Invincibly gullible. Implacably—"

"Okay, okay. You made your point. So what?"

"You still do not understand what I am saying?"

"No!" Remo fumed.

"I have always liked that quality about you."

"That I don't understand half your lessons?"

"No, that you are gullible. A less-gullible man would have run away the day of the logs. A less-gullible man would have refused to enter the room of tiny fires. A less-gullible man would learn to question my assurances and perhaps think for himself. At that stage in your Sinanju training, thinking would have been dangerous, possibly fatal. Fortunately, you did not think. You obeyed. You believed. You acted. And so you lived."

Remo lifted a forefinger and made circles in the air.

"Whooppee shit," he said.

Chiun sighed. "I have trained your body but neglected your mind. I thought you would learn to think. You have not. You continue to be gullible, gullible and trusting."

"You just said it saved my life."

"Indeed. But I do not wish you to be gullible and trusting in all things forever."

"Yeah? So what?"

"And another thing I have neglected. Your religious training."

"I had fantastic religious training."

"If you took to Sinanju the way you took to your religious training, we would not be here now. You would be somewhere swilling beer and eating cow meat. And you would be fat. Grossly fat."

"Says you," said Remo. But he swallowed as if hungry. Chiun wondered if it was the memory of the burned patties of dung Americans called hamburgers or the aroma of fresh rice coming to a boil. Chiun could not tell.

"Normally a Korean child is taught about the Supreme Creator before his fourth birthday. With you, you had already seen over twenty summers and were fixed in your beliefs, even if you no longer embraced them."

"I don't think you've ever told me about the Korean religious system."

"Because it would only confuse you. In Sinanju, we do not teach our young the Korean beliefs. Only Sinanju beliefs."

"So, tell me."

"It is very simple. There is the Supreme Creator, and—"

"What is he called?"

"The Supreme Creator."

"You don't have a name for him? Like Ralph? Or Chong?"

"That is impertinent," said Chiun. "In Sinanju, we do not presume to know his name, so we call him the Supreme Creator, for that is what he is."

"Not even God?"

"Even that is a name. No, we do not call him that. He is the Supreme Creator. He created everything, including the wisest, noblest, most humble, thoughtful, and intelligent creature ever to grace the earth with his tread . . ."

Chiun paused before he completed the sentence.

"The Korean," Remo and Chiun said in the same breath.

Chiun smiled at Remo's perceptiveness.

Remo frowned at Chiun's bigotry.

"I have never told you how the Supreme Creator created the first Korean, have I?"

"No, you just told me that every other race was inferior. I think 'duck droppings' was the term used to describe the white, brown, and black races collectively."

"You had to know that at an early stage in your training. So that you understood the gift that was Sinanju was too good for you. It motivated you."

"It disgusted me."

"I will ignore that remark and continue as if you had not made it. Now, when the Supreme Creator gazed down upon his world, he saw a land of great bounty, of plentiful fruits, of purest water. And he called that good land—"

"Korea," Remo sighed.

Chiun smiled, even if Remo had interrupted him.

Remo glowered.

"And seeing that this land was so rich and peaceful," Chiun went on happily, "the Supreme Creator descended upon Korea. And as he walked along, he met a tiger and a bear. And the tiger and the bear beheld the shape of the Supreme Creator's being and asked to be made like him, to stand upright on their hind legs and to use their forepaws for grasping objects. And the Supreme Creator thought on this and said to them: 'If you will go to that cave beyond the next hill and wait for one hundred days, I will consider you worthy of this gift.'

"And so they went. But the cave was dark, and its walls dripped cold water. And so the tiger departed after only a few days. But the bear stayed. And when, at the end of one hundred days, the Supreme Creator came to the cave, he found the bear alone, cold, and wet and waiting for him."

"He turned the bear into a man?"

"No. Into a woman. And seeing that this woman was fair, he mated with her. And they had a son. And that son was Tangun, the first Korean. This was ten thousand years ago, and since then, all time in Korea dates from the first day Tangun walked upright."

"That is a silly story," snapped Remo.

"And I suppose you whites have a more magnificent origin."

"Yeah, we do. Adam and Eve. God created Adam and then he created Eve from Adam's rib. This took place in the Garden of Eden, where there was plenty of food and the sun always shone."

"From a rib? Oh, Remo, you are so funny. At least my story has a basis in plausibility. In my story, the Supreme Creator did not work with spare parts like some greasy-fingered white mechanic."

The Master of Sinanju slapped his bony knees. His hazel eyes twinkled merrily. His frail body shook with glee.

"That isn't the full story," Remo said heatedly. "And then Adam and Eve mated and produced two sons, Cain and Abel. Cain slew Abel."

"Typical," clucked Chiun. "Even with an entire garden to themselves and plenty of food, they could not get along. How white."

"I'm not sure how much of it I actually believe," Remo admitted grudgingly.

"Oh? Is this a dent in the mighty armor of your faith?" demanded Chiun.

"I said I wasn't sure. That's the Bible story. There are scientific theories too."

"If you are going to tell me the monkey story," said

Chiun, "I may have to leave the room to spare your white feelings."

"I read an article in a scientific magazine once. These scientists claimed that by analyzing human chromosomes or something they had figured out that all human life on earth could be traced back to one woman who had lived in Africa millions of years ago."

"One woman?"

"One woman."

"All life?" demanded Chiun.

"All life," repeated Remo firmly. "It's been proven. Scientifically."

"They must not have tested any Koreans. Our people are only ten thousand years old. And we did not come from Africa."

"All life," Remo said again.

"And you believed this?"

"Scientifically proven."

"If this is so, how did that woman get there?"

Remo looked doubtful. "The article didn't say," he admitted.

"Did it say how this one woman who came before all others came to be with child?"

"No. It didn't."

"Maybe the Supreme Creator took her rib and then created the first man. You whites are always getting your history backwards."

"That's not funny. And just because they left out a few details doesn't mean they haven't proven their case."

"They left out two important details like that and you accepted all the rest of their nonsense! Remo, you are too much. You will believe anything. Even Reverend Sluggard's chicanery."

"I haven't made up my mind about him. Yet."

"And I have not finished telling you the religious beliefs of Sinanju."

"I'm listening."

"I have told you about the Supreme Creator. He

lives in a place called the Void. When Koreans die, they cast off their broken bodies and join him in the Void."

Remo waited. "What else?"

"Else? What else can there be?"

"What about heaven and hell?"

"Silly stories created by unholy holy men to manipulate other men."

"What about sin?"

"That is a priest's word," Chiun spat. "We believe that a man makes mistakes. If they are little mistakes, he will learn from them. If they are big mistakes, he will naturally pay for the consequences of his actions within his lifetime."

"What about forgiveness?"

"The Supreme Creator does not hold grudges."

"What about Jesus?"

"What about Buddha? And Mohammed? And Zoroaster? And Shiva?"

"Don't confuse me with tales of Shiva. I asked about Jesus."

Chiun shrugged. "A carpenter. A rabble-rouser. We had a contract on him at one time, but something more important came up. By the time my ancestor got around to him, he was already dead."

"I was raised to believe he was the Son of God."

"And Masters of Sinanju are taught to do business with kings, not their princes."

"You've got a cockamamie religious system, you know that?"

"Cockamamie?"

"It's too . . . too . . ."

"Simple?" asked Chiun.

"Yeah. Too simple."

"Simplicity is perfection, and perfection, simplicity. The Supreme Creator knew what he was doing. Now I see that the rice is ready. Will you have some?"

"Do you have enough?" Remo asked, eyeing the boiling pot hungrily.

"No, but I am willing to sacrifice."

"I don't want to take all your rice," Remo protested.

"It is a small sacrifice."

Remo hesitated. Finally he said, "Well, okay. But not too much."

And Chiun smiled to himself. Remo had forgotten the white woman with the lascivious mouth. It was as it was written in the Book of Sinanju: "A female is but a female, but rice is a meal." He had once shared that mighty insight with Remo, but Remo had claimed it was a corruption of a white saying having to do with smoking tobacco weeds, another filthy white habit.

18

They came from all over America. By bus and bicycle, by jet, and on foot.

From Maine, from Texas, from California, even from faraway Alaska. Their hair was short and it hung to their shoulder blades. They wore ties and cufflinks and earrings and spiked collars. Some carried expensive luggage in both hands and others only pocket change. They were young and naive, yet hard beyond their years. They were polite and profane. But the one thing they all had in common was that they cried for blood. Moslem blood.

"It's a mob!" cried Reverend Eldon Sluggard, watching them pour through the gates of the Eldon Sluggard World Ministries from the wheelhouse of his luxury yacht.

"No." Victoria Hoar smiled. "It's an army. Our army."

"Where are we going to put 'em all?" Eldon Sluggard moaned. "How are we gonna feed 'em all. You got any idea how much teenagers eat? This is the sixth day of this. Ah never imagined this kind of response."

"We'll find room," Victoria said. She consulted a clipboard containing sheafs of paper. "According to my figures, we're getting a seventy-percent sign-up rate. That's after we weed out the party-seekers with psychological-evaluation tests."

"Are you sure that seventy percent is solid? Ah don't want any more chicken-livered ones like that Booe boy."

"We've improved the tests since the first Crusade. If

these numbers hold up, we'll be up to division strength inside of a week."

"Well," said Eldon Sluggard, watching his security people work the crowd, "Ah hope we don't go broke feeding 'em before we ship 'em out."

Out by the gates, Eldon Sluggard's uniformed security people, under the watchful eyes of Remo and Chiun, were frisking the incoming recruits, confiscating bottles of liquor and, in some cases, firearms. A guard took a twelve-gauge shotgun from one blond boy, and the boy protested. He reached for his weapon. Chiun suddenly appeared behind him and the boy went as stiff as a post and keeled over. He was carried off, still stiff. The crowd settled down.

"Our new security boys sure know how to work a crowd. But on mah life, Ah can't figure them out."

"Neither can I. But as long as they do their job and don't get snoopy, I can handle their being here."

"They got another game. Ah can feel it."

"They're not with the government. They don't feel right for FBI plants."

"Ah don't like the old one. He's too smart. Remo is just a mark as far as Ah'm concerned, but the old one makes me damn nervous."

"Uh-huh," Victoria Hoar said absently as she consulted her clipboard again. "They're incredibly good and they're here to protect you. What have you to be afraid of?"

"The devil," said Reverend Eldon Sluggard worriedly.

Victoria Hoar looked up suddenly. Her eyebrows inched together. "What did you say?"

"The devil. Ah'm afraid of the devil, and not ashamed to admit it either."

"I thought you were above that superstitious drivel."

"Ah am. Ah don't believe in God. But the devil is different. Ah've had nightmares about him. Ah can feel his hairy hands clutching at mah poor throat sometimes. When Ah wake up, Ah can see him grinnin' at me in the dark. Ah can't see his face, just those white teeth floatin' in the air. When Ah blink, they go away."

"Are you serious?" Victoria drank in Sluggard's uneasy expression. "You *are* serious, aren't you?"

"Sometimes he's tall and green with a short spiky tail. Sometimes he's little and yellow with knowing eyes and long horny claws. Like that old chink."

"Remo says he's Korean."

"He's the devil. Ah had a dream last night. He crawled out from under my bed and sprouted leathery green bat wings. Then he carried me off to hell. Ah woke up sweatin' like a boiled pig, and Ah don't even believe in hell. Ah don't want him near me no more."

Victoria Hoar sighed. "I'll put Remo on you permanently. Chiun can handle everything else. Will that satisfy you?"

"He's Satan!" Reverend Eldon Sluggard repeated.

"Get a grip on yourself. You sound like one of those damned mullahs." Victoria Hoar sighed audibly and returned to her sheets. "We now have sixteen Reverend-Sergeants. They're fully indoctrinated. I think it's safe to take the three oldest and smartest ones and promote them to Reverend-Majors. I'm scheduling a ceremony for tonight at seven."

"Yeah, yeah, good," Reverend Sluggard said distractedly.

"I thought we might rush some of today's recruits through and let them in on the ceremony. Then you can give your little speech."

"Uh-hum."

"They're so pumped up when they come in that I think we can risk processing them faster than before. Besides, with these numbers, I think we're going to have to move them into the Gulf sooner than we planned, before they cool down."

"Right, right."

"Are you listening?" demanded Victoria Hoar, snapping her fingers in Sluggard's ear.

"I wonder . . ." Reverend Sluggard said.

"Yes?"

"Who would send the devil to bodyguard me?"

"Oh, for God's sake!" Victoria Hoar said, tossing her clipboard onto the plush seats. She turned to the captain. "Would you excuse us, please?"

The captain crept away without a word.

"What are you doin'?" Reverend Eldon Sluggard asked when he realized that nimble fingers were unbuttoning his Bermuda shorts.

"Your brain is full of cobwebs," Victoria said sharply. "I'm going to blow it clean."

"What? Oh!" said Reverend Eldon Sluggard when he felt his underwear descend.

The last of the new volunteers had slipped through the gates and Remo was ordering them closed when he noticed Victoria Hoar approach.

"Hi!" she said, flashing him an open smile. "Been avoiding me?"

"Um, no," Remo said. "I've been busy."

"Well, you're going to be busier. Reverend Sluggard has decided that you're going to be his personal bodyguard from now on."

"What about Chiun? We've been switching off."

"He'll continue with grounds security. But with the volunteers coming in so fast, Reverend Sluggard feels you should be at his side at all times."

"I don't blame him. Some of these kids are pretty rowdy."

"So I noticed," Victoria Hoar said dryly.

"What kind of kids show up at a religious retreat armed and drunk?"

"Reverend Sluggard is reaching out to the troubled youth of our times. It's only natural that we'd get some of the dregs, the junkies, the petty hoodlums. But don't worry. After a few days at our Christian Campground, they'll be marching to the drumbeat of the Lord."

"Where is this campground?" Remo asked. "I noticed you've been busing them out of here every day."

Victoria Hoar frowned. Why was Remo asking these questions? His face was not as open as it had been. He seemed more focused.

"It's downriver. Don't worry. You'll get to see it. Reverend Sluggard is giving a talk there tonight."

"I'll be interested in hearing it," Remo said levelly.

"Actually, you may not get the chance," Victoria said quickly. "You'll probably be guarding the building."

"A bodyguard usually guards the body, not the house that houses the body," Remo recited.

"What?"

"One of Chiun's sayings, loosely translated. It means that if I'm to do my job, I should stick close to Reverend Sluggard."

"Good point. But we're more concerned about Iranian assassins, not unruly volunteers."

"Whatever you say. I guess I'd better tell Chiun," Remo said, walking back to the gate, where the Master of Sinanju stood watching the approach road as darkness began to seep into the air like billowing ink from an octopus.

Victoria Hoar watched him go. Since that first day, only a week ago, she had subjected Remo to the daily attention of her flirting sexuality. Much to her surprise, she found herself attracted to Remo. There was something about him, some animal magnetism that was so subtle that Remo himself didn't seem aware of it. She had decided that she would sleep with him. Out of curiosity more than desire. And with luck, she would learn his true purpose, if any.

But suddenly Remo hadn't seemed as interested in her as he had been. It was puzzling. Who was playing whom? she wondered as she strode back to the docked *Mary Magdalene*.

"Change in plan," Remo told Chiun. "I've been assigned to guard Sluggard."

"And what will I be doing?" Chiun asked tightly.

"You stick with security control."

"That man shows ridiculous judgment, choosing an assistant Master to guard his person. Does he not know who we are?"

"No, and let's keep it that way," Remo said. "Tonight he's giving a speech at that Christian Campground we've been hearing about. I'm supposed to be there."

"It is possible that the answers Smith seeks are to be found there."

"That's what I'm thinking," Remo said seriously.

"And your feelings toward this Sluggard? Are they any clearer?"

"Whoever or whatever he is, the Iranians hate him enough to come gunning for him. That still keeps him in the good-guy column as far as I'm concerned."

"Pah! At least your attitude has improved," Chiun said unhappily. "Perhaps I can find time to accompany you to this Camp of Christians."

"Too risky. Just stick to headquarters. In case there's an attack, we want prisoners for interrogation."

"Done," said Chiun. "And how was your talk with the harlot Victoria?"

"Who?" Remo asked vaguely, his eyes on the wheelhouse of the boat, where Reverend Sluggard was snoring peacefully, his shorts down around his ankles.

The Master of Sinanju allowed himself a secret self-satisfied smile.

19

Rashid Shiraz drove across the U.S.-Canada border without incident. In the strangely named city of Burlington, Vermont, he boarded a plane for the more strangely named Savannah, Georgia.

Lamar Booe sat quietly beside him on the flight. He spoke only once, to complain about the food. Rashid heard other passengers complain about the food. He could not understand it. Compared to the food of his native Iran, it was wonderful fare. He even asked for seconds.

By the time he landed in Savannah, Rashid Shiraz had lost his earlier fear about traveling through America. He was not harassed by the men, and the women were beautiful. But he refused to allow himself to become complacent. His was a dangerous mission. Capture would mean terrible things. Although he imagined the prison food would not be bad.

In the Savannah airport terminal, he looked around for the contact he was told would be waiting for him. He was not given a description, but was simply told that he would recognize his contact.

And he did. There was a handsome bearded Iranian in black accosting almost everyone who passed him. He showed them pages from a book of some kind. Was the man a fool? Rashid wondered. Was it possible that he was showing Rashid's picture in an effort to locate him?

Grabbing Lamar Booe by the shoulder, Rashid quickly intercepted the Iranian between accostings.

"*Rahe kojast shomaal?*" Rashid whispered the agreed-upon code hotly. "Which way is north?"

"*Ma baradar has team. Wallahi!*" came the countersign. "We are brothers. It is written."

"It is written that you are an idiot!" Rashid hissed back. "Why do you call attention to yourself so?"

"Look," said the contact, displaying his open book.

Rashid saw photographs of mullahs executing Iranian citizens. There was a petition calling for the overthrow of the Grand Ayatollah. Many signatures had been collected.

"Who would suspect an antirevolutionary agitator of being a spy?" the man said, smiling. "Come, a car awaits us."

Hours later, Rashid found himself sitting in a bus filled with other Iranians. His contact man, whose name was Majid, drove. The bus had been rented at the suggestion of Lamar Booe, who sat huddled in the back, his eyes burning with hatred with every mile that took them closer to the place of Reverend Sluggard.

"Every day buses like this go to gate of Sluggard," Majid said. "They are filled with rowdy young men."

"Not like these," Rashid grinned wolfishly, waving at the passengers. Every Iranian carried a weapon. Their kaffiyehs were in their pockets.

They pulled up short of the gates. The gates were closed.

"We could ram gate," Majid suggested.

"I have a better idea," said Rashid, drifting back to where Lamar Booe sat.

"You recognize where we are, Cross-Worshipper?" he asked.

Lamar Booe nodded.

"We have come to the time when you repay the benevolent Islamic Republic of Iran for your worthless life. Can you get them to open the gate?"

"Yes," Lamar Booe whispered. He was staring at the floor, his eyes hollow.

"If you do this, you will not be harmed. We guarantee this. We only want to capture this Sluggard."

Lamar Booe stood up. He looked Rashid Shiraz straight in the eye.

"Not if I get to him first," he said in a dead voice. His shaking hands gripped an imaginary object tightly. Rashid made a mental note to make certain that Lamar Booe didn't get his hands on Reverend Sluggard's throat. He doubted all the force in the universe could pry them loose.

20

Remo Williams was standing guard at the door of Reverend Eldon Sluggard's shipboard quarters when Chiun descended the companionway attired in a simple saffron kimono.

"Problem?" Remo asked.

"I bear glad news for the Sluggard."

"The Reverend Sluggard," Remo corrected. "Calling him the Sluggard is disrespectful."

Chiun shrugged. "Lamar Booe has returned to the Sluggard's flock," he reported.

"Great. Who's he?"

"Do you not remember, Remo? The missing boy. The one whose parents claim that he never returned from this place."

"Oh, right. Reverend Sluggard will be happy to hear it."

"Then why do you not knock on his door?"

"He asked not to be disturbed. Victoria is there with him. They're having a prayer session. It's been very quiet, but they should be out any minute. We're casting off for the Christian Campground soon."

"I see," said Chiun, pushing Remo aside. He looked into the keyhole of the great door. He did not have to bend very far to see.

"Chiun. That's snooping!"

"Information gathering," Chiun shot back. He moved this way and that, trying to see.

"It's our jobs if you're caught," Remo said in a resigned voice.

When Chiun suddenly withdrew from the keyhole, a look of disgust etched on his wrinkled features, Remo asked, "Had enough?"

"Judge for yourself," Chiun said, stepping aside.

Reluctantly Remo looked. He saw Victoria Hoar's back. She was on her knees facing Reverend Sluggard. One meaty hand rested on her head, the other flailed the air. Reverend Sluggard's face was reddening by the second. His eyes were squinched shut as if in pain.

"Well?" Chiun demanded after Remo stepped back from the keyhole.

"Well what?" Remo asked. "He's leading her in prayer."

"Who is leading whom is another question," Chiun snapped. "But of one thing I am certain, you are as blind as the Sluggard is disgusting."

"Reverend Sluggard. And I don't know what you're talking about. So why don't you tell them to bring the kid here? I'm sure Reverend Sluggard will want to talk to him when he's done."

"Men like him are never done." And with that cryptic remark, the Master of Sinanju stamped up to the deck.

Minutes later, when Remo heard talking coming from the other side of the door, he decided it was a good time to break the wonderful news to Reverend Sluggard. He knocked loudly.

"What is it?" Reverend Sluggard snarled. "Ah said Ah was not to be disturbed."

"Great news," Remo called back.

There was a flurry of sounds and Reverend Sluggard's face appeared through a crack in the door. His jowly face was flushed, his hair unkempt.

"Did we nuke Ah-ran?"

"No. Lamar Booe's back," Remo said cheerily. "Isn't that wonderful?"

Reverend Eldon Sluggard's face did not register pleasure. At first it registered a kind of dazed blankness. Then, as the name sank in, his blank expression started to come apart. The mouth went slack. The eyes grew wild. His nostrils dilated explosively and Reverend Sluggard's hand on the door edge turned so white his many rings seemed to flush with added color.

"Whaaaa—" he said.

"Lamar Booe. The kid whose parents are suing you. He says it's all a big misunderstanding. He wants to see you."

"Whaaaa—" Reverend Sluggard said again.

"Lamar Booe," Remo said, frowning. "He—"

"Ah know who he is!" Reverend Sluggard snapped. "Don't let him in. Ah don't want to see his cowardly face. Stop him!"

"But Chiun's bringing him aboard."

"What is the problem?" asked Victoria Hoar.

"That Booe boy. He's back!" Sluggard's voice was hoarse.

"Back? How can he be back? He was with the others?"

"Someone's at the gate sayin' he's him."

"I don't get it," Remo said. "I thought you'd be pleased."

"Tell the captain to cast off now!" Sluggard ordered.

"But—"

"Now!" Reverend Sluggard screamed. "Don't you understand the word 'now'?"

Frowning, Remo went to the wheelhouse and relayed the order.

Immediately, white-uniformed crewmen began to cast off lines. The great dual diesel engines began to turn.

When Remo, his head shaking in confusion, returned to the deck, he saw that Chiun was directing the uniformed guards to open the electrically controlled gates to the Eldon Sluggard World Ministries.

A lone boy walked in. The gate started to close after him. Chiun went to greet the boy, when, suddenly, a bus gunned up the street, executed a sharp veer, and skidding on three wheels, rammed the gate. The gate halves, not fully closed, went flying. One cracked the windshield and bounced away. The other went under the front tires as if swallowed by a voracious maw.

The bus bore down on Lamar Booe. The boy turned. And froze.

Remo, knowing he was too far away to affect what would happen next, looked for Chiun. But Chiun wasn't at the spot he had been. Remo's gaze returned to the bus. He caught sight of a flash of saffron. And Lamar Booe was carried out of the way of the juggernaut of a bus.

"Atta boy, Chiun!" Remo shouted.

The bus plowed into the quadrangle. It snapped the standing cross in two and only then skidded to a halt. The door flew open and dozens of men in kaffiyehs and faded dungarees stormed out of the bus. Their weapons, an assortment of machine pistols and automatic rifles, erupted all at once.

The cacophony of shooting and screaming reminded Remo of Vietnam.

Reverend Sluggard stomped up from below.

"What's going on?" he thundered.

Remo opened his mouth to speak, but the sight of Reverend Sluggard stopped him. Reverend Sluggard wore a greenish-gold uniform. Gold braid decorated his epaulets. He wore a pristine white visored cap and a ceremonial sword in a scabbard. His ample chest was decorated with rows of military-style ribbons. But they were unlike any service decorations Remo had ever seen. Reverend Sluggard's chest looked like a circuit board. Remo saw crosses, circles and other arcane designs, including one that at a glance seemed to read "Order of the Wrath of the Lord."

"Reverend Sluggard . . ." Remo said dumbfoundedly.

"Reverend-General Sluggard," he boomed proudly. "When Ah'm in uniform, Ah'm Reverend-General Sluggard, the Lord's fearless right arm. "Now, what's goin' on?"

"Iranians," Remo said, pointing.

Reverend-General Eldon Sluggard clutched his sword hilt. "How . . . how can you tell?" he croaked.

"See those checkered things over their heads? That makes them Middle Easterners. Probably Iranians."

"Tell them to cast off."

"I did."

"Well, tell 'em to cast off faster. We got to get out of here!" The Lord's fearless right arm looked around frantically. He spied a bullhorn on a deck hook and yanked it to his face.

"Cast off! Cast this tub off! Hurry!" Then he turned his attention to the quadrangle. People were pouring out of the ministry buildings. Staff members. When they saw uniformed guardsmen fall, they retreated. Some of the new recruits stood frozen in uncertainty.

"You, there! Boys!" Reverend-General Sluggard howled. "Take up your swords and smite them shitty Moslems!"

A few of the braver volunteers started forward. They were cut down by a precision stream of fire.

"Let Chiun and me handle this," Remo said, starting over the rail.

"Don't be a fool. They're cannon fodder. And I need you here."

"And Chiun needs my help," Remo said. He hit the dock with no more sound than a paper cup and pelted toward the quadrangle.

Remo came around the corner of the Temple of Tribute, whose glass walls were already shattered from stray rounds, and paused long enough to fix Chiun's position. Chiun was slipping up from the gate. Remo backtracked him with his eyes and saw that the boy, Lamar Booe, was safely in one of the glass gate boxes where Chiun had left him. The boy was pounding to get out. The

expression on his face was so frightened it looked to
Remo like anger, not fear.

Remo caught Chiun's attention with a wave. He raised
two fingers in the old V-for-victory sign. He hoped
Chiun would recognize the signal for a double Scarlet
Ribbon.

Remo had no time to wait. He began to run. He cut
left, then right, not seeking shelter from the rounds
that were flying in all directions, sickling leaves from
trees and chopping the Spanish moss that decorated the
eucalyptus. Remo picked up speed until he was moving
in a weaving pattern known to old Masters of Sinanju as
the Scarlet Ribbon.

Bullets flew around his head and feet. No one aiming
could possibly hit him, Remo knew, because by the
time they lined up on him, he was already moving out
of target position. His only fear, strangely enough, was
from wild ricochets. But as he wove the beginnings of
the ribbon, his mind was free of all fear, all doubt. He
was at one with the situation.

The ribbon started to gain color when Remo encountered his first opponent. He took him out with a slash-
ing side kick to the testicles. Another terrorist spotted
him, and Remo paused a half-step, whirled, and as the
man opened fire, came up under the bullet track and
slapped his larynx loose. He went down gurgling. The
dying man's wild fire caused another terrorist behind
Remo to scream in agony. His screams attracted the
attention of the other terrorists and Remo became the
focus of that attention.

Which was exactly what he wanted.

It was then that the Scarlet Ribbon truly turned
scarlet.

Remo moved in and out between his attackers. A
thrust here. A flying kick there. He lunged for a man
who was frantically pulling an empty clip from a Mac
10. Remo yanked a full clip from the man's belt and

jammed it into the man's cloth-covered mouth, spiking him to the side of the bullet-riddled bus.

Others, seeing him pause in mid-action, trained their weapons on him. Triggers were pressed. The crossfire missed Remo, who flashed into action again. It got several terrorists. For that was what the Scarlet Ribbon was designed to do—turn the fury of a large force upon its members with killing result.

Remo resumed his furious running. Halfway through the ribbon, he streaked by the Master of Sinanju.

"Sluggard's taken off in a panic," Remo said.

"His kind always does," returned Chiun as he executed a Heron Drop. He flashed into the air, seemed to hang in space like a dandelion seed settling to earth, and while streams of fire converged on the spot where he floated, his sandaled feet, spreading, came down on the heads of two terrorists fighting at close quarters. Two necks collapsed like empty soda cans. Vertebrae shattered audibly. Chiun alighted delicately and moved on.

Rashid Shiraz saw his bullets miss the old Oriental once again. He saw him break two of his fellow Iranians' necks. He sighted on the Oriental again. He missed. He missed again. He reloaded. And in the precious seconds between pulling out the empty clip and snapping in a fresh magazine, three more of his men fell on the grass, their blood staining the ground.

Rashid turned his attention back to the white man. He was bigger. He would be a better target. But when he looked, he saw his men trying to cut the American down. The man zipped between the bullet tracks crazily. It was an insane maneuver because he was not running away from the bullets, but among them. It was as if he were daring the men to shoot at him.

Instead, the men ended up shooting at one another.

Witnessing his entire force wilting like roses in the summer heat, Rashid felt his courage run down his legs. He ran for the bus, hoping its tires were not punctured. The bus started. He sent it lumbering around and steered for the gaping gate. One gate half was still caught under the chassis. It sparked and rattled, inhibiting speed.

As Rashid barreled toward the entrance, he saw the stupid American boy, Lamar Booe, in the guard box. He sent a spray of bullets into the box. Lamar went down. There must be no one left to talk.

The bus cracked the fieldstone gatepost going around the corner and Rashid floored the gas.

The bus picked up speed slowly. The chassis rattled against the trapped gate. In his right-side mirror Rashid spotted the white American running after the bus.

"Fool!" he spat. And then he noticed that the Oriental was coming up on the left side. He cursed the trapped gate. It was slowing him down so much that even the old one was gaining on the bus.

Rashid kicked at the gas pedal desperately. The speedometer hovered at fifty. He blinked. At fifty they should not be keeping pace. Yet they were.

Rashid, cursing behind his kaffiyeh, sent the bus skittering around. If he could not outrun them, he would run them down.

The bus slammed around. Its sharp turn sent the gate flying. The tires were free. Rashid pushed the accelerator harder.

The two saw him coming. They stopped, side by side in the middle of the road, as he bore down on them. They did not move. Rashid grinned fiercely. Good. They were paralyzed with fear.

Their faces did not look fearful as they filled the windshield, however. They looked resolute. Even fearless. Rashid could see the whites of their eyes now. There was no mistaking their resoluteness. Were they suicidal?

Rashid had no more time to contemplate it. The bus was upon them. He whipped the tail of his kaffiyeh in

front of his face protectively. The impact would certainly shatter the windshield into a million dangerous
pieces. He shut his eyes.

But no sound of impact came. Instead, there was a
double *pop*. Rashid wrestled with the suddenly difficult
wheel. He shook the kaffiyeh free so he could see. The
windshield was intact. And in the rearview mirror he
could see, on either side, the two enemies of Islam
settling to their feet as if they were coming out of
attacking spins.

But what had they been attacking?

When the steering wheel lurched to the right, Rashid
experienced understanding. He had a momentary flash,
like telepathy, that his front tires had burst. Somehow,
he had the wild mental image that the two men had
burst them. He could imagine their flying feet doing
that somehow. He knew it was impossible, but his
mind leapt to that conclusion as if it was the only way it
could correlate what was happening to him.

Then the bus lurched off the road onto the soft shoulder and down the riverbank.

Rashid's face kissed the windshield with shattering
finality and the brackish taste of the river mud fouled
his mouth.

Remo waded into the water, shoved open the folding
doors, and looked in.

"Dead," he called back to Chiun.

"So perish the enemies of Sinanju," Chiun said firmly.

"You mean the enemies of Reverend Sluggard," Remo
said, returning to the roadside. "And he was probably
the only one who could tell us what's going on."

"Perhaps one of the others lived."

"After a double Scarlet Ribbon? We'll be lucky if
their fingerprints survived."

"True," said Chiun. "Although I noticed that during
the first stage of the attack, your elbow was bent."

"It was not."

"Slightly."

"No way."

"Just a hair."

"Let's see if the Booe kid is alive," Remo said, annoyed. "I think he might have something to tell us."

"What makes you say that?"

"Reverend-General Sluggard turned white as a sheet when I mentioned that the kid was back. He was scared shitless."

"Reverend-General?"

"He was wearing a uniform, sword, and all the trimmings."

"Then I was right!" Chiun exclaimed.

"About what?"

"I will tell you after the boy confirms it."

"Why not now so I won't be surprised?"

"You will be surprised in either case. And perhaps then you and Smith will finally learn to heed my wisdom."

"Don't count on it," Remo said.

21

They found Lamar Booe on the floor of the guard box. The floor was a sticky red.

Remo snapped the door off its hinges and knelt over the boy.

"Can you talk, son?" he asked.

The boy's mouth opened. A line of scarlet leaked out of one corner. He gurgled. Remo saw that the ragged hole in his chest bubbled like a little red fountain. He would not live. Remo placed a forefinger over the hole and said gently, "Try."

"Is he dead?" Booe gurgled.

"Yes, we got them all. Were they Iranians?"

"Yes," said Chiun.

"No," Lamar Booe gasped.

"He is clearly delirious," Chiun said. "They were Persians."

"I meant . . . Sluggard," Booe gasped.

"Sluggard? An Iranian?" Remo asked.

"I believe he is trying to learn if the Sluggard is dead. Is that correct, boy?" Chiun asked.

Lamar Booe nodded weakly. His face was drained of color.

"No, he got away," Remo told him.

"Too . . . damn . . . bad."

"What are you saying?" Remo demanded.

"He . . . got me . . . into this," Lamar Booe said in a pain-blurred voice.

"This what?"

"Crusade."

"What about his crusade? What does that have to do with anything?" Remo asked.

Lamar Booe shook his head wearily. No words came.

"He means 'crusade' in the old sense. A holy war," Chiun intoned. "Is that not so?"

Lamar Booe nodded. "I went over with . . . first wave. We were . . . massacred. Iranians. We had no . . . chance. They let me come back only . . . if I led them to . . . Sluggard. Said I'd be set . . . free. They lied. Everyone lied. I only wanted . . . something to believe in."

"A Crusade?" Remo asked. "For what?"

"Nail."

"Must be a hell of a nail," Remo put in.

"From . . . the Cross. Sluggard said . . . nail from Crucifixion. Iranians have it. A rug seller uses it to hold up . . . picture of Ayatollah. Sluggard said it was . . . monstrous blasphemy. Our task was to . . . liberate nail."

"A nail?" Remo repeated, puzzled.

"Whites have launched their holy wars over lesser trifles," Chiun said disdainfully.

"The Holy Nail," Lamar Booe said, his words stronger now. "I carried the banner. We were going to sweep over them, shouting hosannas, until we reached Tehran. Nothing could stop us. We were the Knights of the Lord."

"Who is this carpet seller?" demanded Chiun.

"Masood . . . something."

"When did this happen?" Remo asked.

"Weeks—weeks ago. Seems like years." And under his breath, Lamar Booe of Sapulpa, Oklahoma, began to chant.

"Marq bar Sluggard! Marq bar Sluggard!"

Suddenly the light in Lamar Booe's eyes flared up in pain. Then it died like a dwindling star.

"He's gone," Remo said, closing the boy's eyes with

his fingers. He turned to Chiun. "All this over a nail," he said, looking at the bodies scattered about the quadrangle of the Eldon Sluggard World Ministries.

"No," said Chiun. "It is never over the things they claim. The nail is merely the excuse. This Sluggard wants more."

"Such as?"

"In the old Crusades, they marched on Jerusalem, claiming that it was a holy place being defiled by Moslems. But in truth, they lusted after the wealth of the lands surrounding Jerusalem. Calling it holy was a way to manipulate the gullible. Like this boy. Like such as you who do not outgrow their childhood superstitions."

"We can argue religion later. What do we do now?"

"We follow this Sluggard. It is time to wring some truth from his oily lips."

Remo looked over toward the Wilmington River.

"He's long gone."

"I see a small boat. We will take that. Eventually we will come upon his ship. When we do, we will find the place of his camp."

They found the *Mary Magdalene* docked nearly ten miles downriver. It was deserted. Remo sent the speedboat up onto the muddy riverbank, not bothering to tie it up. They jumped off and followed a gravel path into a moss-draped forest. In a clearing, they found it.

But the Christian Campground was deserted.

"They took off awfully quick. But in what?" Remo looked at the dirt. There were no conspicuous vehicle tracks. Certainly not enough to cart away the thousands of teenage volunteers that had been shipped here.

Chiun pointed out the imprints of many footsteps. They followed them back to the river.

Out on the water there was little traffic. A sloop tacked into the wind. A trawler crossed its wake. Out on the Atlantic a huge black ship moved slowly. Its long low lines and tall white superstructure told Remo that it was an oil tanker. He dismissed it from consideration.

"Now what?" he asked Chiun.

"We go to Persia. Where Smith should have sent us in the first place."

"You think that's where they went?"

"There is no question. Look around you. What do you see?"

"Looks like boot camp. Those long buildings are barracks. That's an obstacle course. Probably a firing range somewhere too."

"Let us find a telephone. I must call Smith."

"You? I thought you were mad at him."

"Mad enough to tell him I told him so," Chiun said firmly.

"Told him what?"

"I spoke with Smith the other day, when I first suspected the true nature of Sluggard's Crusade. Smith dismissed my theory. Now we have proof."

"Oh, really?" Remo said skeptically. "You knew it all along? I'll have to hear that from Smith himself, if you don't mind."

"Then follow me, O ye of little faith," said Chiun, leading the way.

The long low buildings were indeed barracks. They were filled with empty rumpled cots. But no telephones.

Another building housed target-shooting stations. Cardboard cutouts of Middle Eastern terrorists and mullahs in white turbans stood in long rows. They were riddled. The walls behind them were riddled. Even the ceiling was punctured by bullet holes.

Walking through the obstacle course, Remo remarked, "Reminds me of Camp Pendleton."

One building proved to be a headquarters. In a map-covered office, Remo found a telephone. He put in a call to Smith.

"Smitty? Remo. Yeah, it's been a few days. We've been busy. But we got results. You might find them hard to accept, but here it is. Ready for this? Sluggard's launching a Crusade. Yeah, that kind of a Crusade. It's over a nail, believe it or not. Supposed to be from the Crucifixion."

Remo found Chiun tugging on his wrist. "What? Hold it a sec, Smith. What is it?" Remo asked Chiun.

"Ask him if he believes me now."

"Right. Smitty, did Chiun brief you on this before? Oh, he did." Remo turned to Chiun. "You were right, Little Father. I apologize for not believing you."

"Does Smith apologize? That is what I wish to know."

"Smith, Chiun wants to know if you're going to apologize for not believing him."

Remo listened. Finally he told Chiun, "Yes, he apologizes."

"Not good enough. I want it in writing."

"Later," Remo said, waving Chiun off. "We have to deal with this situation first."

Swiftly Remo related the events of the day, the attack on Sluggard's headquarters, and the departure from the Christian Campground of several thousand hotheaded teenage volunteers.

Remo finished with a growled, "They disappeared into thin air."

"They did not," Chiun put in. "They were on the big boat."

"What big boat?" Remo wanted to know.

"The big black boat. I saw you watching it."

"The oil tanker? Impossible."

"You are very confident for a person who has just apologized for his earlier lack of faith in my awesome powers of deduction."

Remo sighed. "Chiun says they got away on an oil tanker. Feed that to your computers, Smitty."

At Folcroft Sanitarium, Harold W. Smith called up his computer. It was preposterous. The very idea of a modern Crusade against Iran. But Remo had described the so-called Christian Campground. And it fit reports

Smith had been tracking of other parents whose children never returned from Sluggard's Christian retreat.

"Did you get the name of the ship?" he asked into the phone.

"Afraid not," said Remo.

"Yes," came Chiun's squeaky voice.

"What is it?" Smith asked.

Chiun's voice came thinly. "The *Seaworthy Gargantuan*."

"Thank you," Smith said as he began inputting the name. Remo passed along Smith's thanks. Chiun's huffy reply was inaudible.

Smith read the file aloud when it came up. "The *Seaworthy Gargantuan* is owned by the Mammoth Oil and Shale Recovery Corporation of McAllen, Texas. They're big. Or they were before the Texas oil collapse. Hmmmm. What is this?" he muttered. A flag light was blinking. Smith hit a key.

Up came a file on a ship registered to the same firm, the *Seawise Behemoth*.

"Listen to this, Remo," Smith said excitedly. "The *Seaworthy Gargantuan* is a sister ship to the tanker that was seized by the Iranians over a week ago, the *Seawise Behemoth*. According to my sources, the Iranians claim it was on some kind of espionage mission and they are holding it until they get reparations. We assumed it was another of their strange political games, but I'm beginning to see a pattern, aren't you? Remo? Remo?"

"What?" Remo said. "Sorry, Smith. I was looking at this wall map."

"Please pay attention. This is important."

"So is this. You ever hear of the Pershing Gulf?"

"Persian. Look closer."

"I am and I see the Pershing Gulf. And next to it the Kingdom of Sluggard. Where Iraq should be is Victoria-land. And I think Eldon Island is what normal people call Kharg Island, where the Iranians ship out a lot of their oil."

"My God. Then it's true."

"It's crazy, is what it is," Remo muttered, "I see a lot of red arrows and lines on the coast. They look like lines of attack. This circle must be a beachhead. Could be where they expect to land. It's just up from the Strait of Griselda. Who the hell is Griselda, I wonder?"

"Obviously that is the Strait of Hormuz. I think the best course of action is for you and Chiun to be there to meet them on the beach."

"Why bother?" Remo asked. "The way I see it, we don't have a downside. If the Iranians wipe out Sluggard, all the better. If it goes the other way, I'm not going to cry over a few less Revolutionary Guards."

"Have you forgotten the terrorist attacks that came in the wake of Sluggard's first move—for obviously that is what has triggered this entire crisis. Another attack means more terror for us. And Sluggard's actions are in violation of the Neutrality Act forbidding U.S. citizens from making war on a foreign power. His Crusaders are innocent dupes. Your job, Remo is to prevent Sluggard from attacking Iran and to neutralize his army. Failing that, you are to eliminate Sluggard and somehow convince the Iranians that he is not acting on behalf of the United States, either officially or unofficially."

"Convincing the Iranians will have to be Chiun's department," Remo said reluctantly. "All right, we're on. Got any idea how you're going to get us there?"

"Er, no," Smith admitted hesitantly. "Actually, this could be difficult."

"Well, at least Chiun will be happy. He's getting what he wants."

"And what is that?" Chiun asked distantly.

"Smith says we're going to Iran."

"Persia! Ah, I can taste the tender melons now."

"And I can smell the blood," Remo said. "Any ideas

about how to get us there?" he asked Chiun. "Smith says he's stumped."

"Why, it is simple. As Masters of Sinanju, we will use our diplomatic impunity."

Smith, hearing Chiun's words, protested, "But I can't arrange diplomatic immunity for you and Chiun. We're in a state of low-intensity war with Iran."

"Chiun didn't say 'immunity.' He said 'impunity.' "

"What does that mean?" Smith asked.

"It means," Remo returned, "that I wouldn't want to be the Iranian who tries to get in Chiun's way."

22

The supertanker *Seaworthy Gargantuan* plowed the waves under a full moon.

Reverend-General Eldon Sluggard paced the afterdeck.

"Where is that bitch?" he raged.

Finally Victoria Hoar came down the deck, her high heels clicking. Her long hair danced behind her like a horse's tail.

"Ah been askin' for you," he said. "Ah been tryin' to talk sense to the captain, but he won't turn this scow around."

"Not possible," Victoria Hoar said simply. "We're on course for Iran."

"Ah-ran!" Reverend-General Sluggard screeched. "Ah ain't goin' to raghead land."

"Yes, you are. It's your job to keep up the morale of your Cross Crusaders."

"Who's Reverend-General around here anyway?"

"You. But this ship is sailing under my orders."

"It is? I thought you said your daddy ran this oil company. Well, Ah want to talk with him."

"You'd need a Ouija board. He died. Heart attack. When they plugged up the best well he ever drilled down in Hidalgo County, Texas, it killed him. I run the company now."

"Ah smell a setup. You had this tub waiting all along."

"I didn't expect to move this soon, but here we are."

"Ah can't go to Ah-ran. You know what they'll do to me if Ah'm taken prisoner."

"Don't get taken prisoner," Victoria Hoar said.

Reverend-General Eldon Sluggard turned red. "You been playin' me right along, ain't you? Like an old fiddle."

"More like a saxophone. And you hit every note. Now, let me suggest you start practicing for when you hit the beach."

"When mah Cross Crusaders hit the beach, you mean."

"When they hit the beach under your charge. I didn't want to tell you before this, but remember when I said I'd figured out what had gone wrong the first time? That last Crusade didn't have a truly inspiring leader. This time, it will. You."

"No damn way."

"I'd put that silver-tongued voice of yours to work," Victoria Hoar went on, indifferent to Reverend-General Sluggard's rantings. "Because you're going to be the first to hit the beach, like it or not. And you'd better have a well-motivated force backing you up, or you're going to be out there all alone."

The thought settled onto Reverend-General Sluggard's beefy face.

"If Ah could swim . . ." he said gratingly.

"But you can't," returned Victoria Hoar, turning on her heel and stalking off.

"Bitch," called Reverend-General Eldon Sluggard. And this time he did not say it under his breath.

A mocking laugh floated back to him.

23

General Adnan Mefki entered the Grand Ayatollah's private garden, his face set.

The Grand Ayatollah looked up from his raisin-sweetened tea and signed for the general to speak. The soft winds coming down off the Elburz Mountains sent the baskets of red roses rippling, filling the air with their perfumy sweetness.

"I have word that a delegation from the House of Sinanju desires an audience with your holiness."

"I know of no such place," the Grand Ayatollah said distantly.

"Sinanju is a village in North Korea, Imam, the seat of a powerful sect of assassins. They serviced the former shahs and before them, the caliphs of old Persia. I have known of this house all my life. Many believed them extinct."

"I will not treat with any emissary who consorted with the infidel shahs. Do not allow them to enter this country."

"I am afraid it is too late. They are in Tehran. I do not know how. The ways of Sinanju are most mysterious. But they have sent word that they will be here within the hour and they expect an audience."

"And who are they to make demands of us?" asked the Grand Ayatollah.

The general paused, his expression dumbfounded. Although no Master of Sinanju had set foot in Iran in generations, some years ago the latest Master of Sinanju had done a kindness for the last shah. Sinanju could not be denied.

"They," the general said at last, as if it explained everything, "are Sinanju."

And in the distance, the melting ice of the Elburz Mountains cracked like a thunderclap.

The Master of Sinanju strolled down the center of Lalehzar Street. His carriage was straight. His face lifted proudly.

"See how the crowds part for us here?" Chiun said loftily. "The past service rendered by my ancestors has not been forgotten."

"No offense, Little father," Remo said, "but I think it was those two Revolutionary Guards you dismembered back there that did the trick."

"Hoodlums," said Chiun. "Ruffians. Obviously uneducated, for they did not recognize me by sight."

"The border guards were the same way. Every checkpoint from here to Pakistan was full of them. Between the two of us, they're going to have to start a new recruitment drive to replenish the ranks. If you ask me, no one bothered to tell them about Sinanju's contributions to Persian culture."

"The rulers will be different. They will greet us with flowers and songs from the old days. Then we will lay Smith's cause before them and this matter will be swiftly settled. Perhaps we will offer as an added incentive to rid this worthy land of these uneducated ruffians."

"I think you'll have to depopulate Iran if you want to do that," said Remo, looking around warily. "And I don't see anything very worthy here. Look at all these destroyed buildings."

"No doubt the new leader is ridding his capital of these unsightly cereal-box buildings. I understand the new leader believes in the old ways."

"Yeah, in stagnation and economic ruin. This place is a dump. And from the looks of things, I'd say Iraq had more to do with the urban renewal than Iran."

"Iraq, too, was once a worthy place. Perhaps we shall visit it next. Ah," cooed Chiun. noticing a sidewalk vendor. "A melon seller. Come, come, Remo, I have waited all my life to break a good Persian melon with you."

"Should we?"

"We have plenty of time before the Sluggard's ship arrives, and our business with the Persian rulers will be swiftly completed."

Chiun floated over to the melon seller's stall. The rough-skinned melons were piled in old crates on the sidewalk. Chiun examined several of them critically, sometimes shaking them close to his ear.

'Find a good one?" Remo asked patiently.

"These are not ripe. It may be earlier in the season than I thought. Ah, here is a choice one. Pay the man, Remo.'

Remo forked over an American twenty-dollar bill. He was not given change.

The Master of Sinanju grasped the melon in both hands. His long-nailed thumbs sank into the skin like hypodermics.

"Better not drop it," Remo cautioned. "That's a twenty-dollar melon."

Chiun separated his hands. With a soft splitting sound, the melon fell into exact halves into his hands. He offered Remo one.

Remo looked at the exposed yellow meat.

"It's all mushy inside," he complained. "Spoiled."

Chiun looked. And saw that it was so. Angrily he took the melon back to the proprietor. Remo watched as a heated exchange in Farsi ensued. It ended with Chiun going through all the melons, splitting them in half, and dropping them in the gutter, where they splashed in their overripeness. The melon seller was screaming and tearing at his hair.

When Chiun returned to Remo's side, he said, "Recover your money. He has no good melons."

"Must be a ripoff artist," Remo said, not bothering to go after his twenty dollars. It was out of Smith's pocket anyway.

They walked until they came to a pistachio vendor. Chiun's sullen face lit up.

"The pistachios look good," he said brightly. But when he examined the tall paper bags filled to the brim, he saw that they were small, wizened nuts, not the fat green ones his ancestors had described.

His face darkening, Chiun resumed his stride.

"This place has fallen upon evil days," he muttered. "The melons are bad and the pistachios are not worth the trouble it took to harvest them. What could have happened?"

"They happened," said Remo, jerking a thumb at a pair of passing white-turbaned mullahs. They stalked down the street in their camel-hair cloaks like buzzards with folded wings.

At the Iranian Parliament building, General Mefki greeted the Master of Sinanju with a proper bow. Not a full bow, but a respectful one, Chiun noted.

"We will see your leader now," Chiun told him.

"A thousand pardons," returned the general, his face shiny with sweat. "But the Grand Ayatollah has declined to see you. I have tried to reason with him, but—"

The general's words stopped at the sight of the change in the Master of Sinanju's face. It was stormy, the eyes afire.

"I've seen that expression before," Remo said in English. "I'd drag your High Ayatollah out by the beard if I were you."

"Come with me," said the general, who suddenly feared a firing squad less than he did the fire in the tiny Korean's eyes.

The Grand Ayatollah looked up sharply from his prayer rug on the floor. His eyes narrowed at the sight of the pair whom the general had escorted into his private chamber of meditation.

"In the name of Allah the Compassionate, the Merciful," he mumbled.

"What is this he mutters?" Chiun asked.

"The Ayatollah is very pious," said General Mefki. "He asks for Allah's guidance at the beginning of all meetings."

"He'd better pray this one goes right," Remo said. The general looked at him as if suddenly placing the accent. "American?" he asked.

"Yes," said Remo.

"No," said Chiun. "He is Sinanju. He used to be American."

"But you work for America now?"

This exchange obviously puzzled the Grand Ayatollah, who did not speak English. He asked a question of the general.

Chiun answered it, in perfect Farsi.

"I am Chiun, reigning Master of Sinanju. My ancestors were once proud to have served the Peacock Throne."

The Grand Ayatollah took a sip of his tea. He spat at Chiun's feet in a gesture of contempt. In Farsi he intoned, "The shah was a wounded serpent, as were all who came before him. If you served his ilk, that makes you a serpent's lackey."

Chiun's face trembled, and Remo wondered if he should get between Chiun and the Grand Ayatollah. Then he recalled Smith's instructions.

"Remember, Smith wants us to avoid a war here," he whispered.

Chiun hesitated. His face went flat.

"I come as an emissary of the United States," Chiun said quietly, evenly. And he was surprised to see the Ayatollah's face betray a flicker of fear.

"He fears America, not Sinanju," Chiun whispered to Remo.

"Obviously he doesn't know Sinanju from Shinola," Remo whispered back. "Keep that in mind."

"A force of American renegades has set sail for these shores," Chiun went on. "These people are hosts of a man named Sluggard. It is not the wish of the American emperor that these forces inflict harm upon Persia. Nor is it America's wish that these Americans, except possibly their leader, come to harm here. Allow us to arrest our renegades, and the one who has caused you so much trouble, Sluggard, will be turned over to you."

"Hey, I don't think that's a good idea, Chiun," Remo complained when he got the translation. "Sluggard may be bad, but he's still an American. I can't see turning him over to these turban-winders."

"Hush," said Chiun. He turned to the Grand Ayatollah. "Does the Imam agree?"

The Grand Ayatollah said nothing. He took another sip of tea. This time he swallowed it.

General Mefki spoke up then.

"I believe I can assure you that our forces will not engage these Americans, if the House of Sinanju will turn them away."

"Done," said Chiun.

"I will not speak for the Pasdaran," said the Grand Ayatollah at last. "They will do what they will do. It is in Allah's hands."

Chiun's brow furrowed.

"What does that mean?" Remo asked General Mefki after he had translated.

"It is their way of avoiding responsibility," he replied. "The clerics can no longer control the Revolutionary Guards they have inflicted upon this country, but they dare not admit it."

"Tell him," Remo said, gesturing toward the Grand Ayatollah, "that if his Guards cross us, we will crush their bones to powder."

General Mefki translated Remo's words.

The Grand Ayatollah's face betrayed true fear then. And Chiun was so shocked he said nothing.

Finally the Grand Ayatollah began muttering inaudibly.

"We will sink the American fleet in the Gulf. We will punish the Great Satan, here and on its very shores."

"He's bluffing," General Mefki explained in English. "They are all like that, revenge-crazed. He is old and helpless and knows it. The mullahs have broken the back of this once-proud nation and it is only a matter of time before the people rise up against them. Let me suggest we end this audience and that you go do what you must. You have my pledge of noninterference. It is all you can hope for here."

Chiun, his face unhappy, strode up to the Grand Ayatollah and, standing almost in his face, bowed low over the man's samovar and piles of cakes.

"May Allah maintain your shadow," he said, and he straightened. "We go now to accomplish our mission."

The Grand Ayatollah waved him away with a feeble gesture.

Outside, on the Parliament steps, Remo asked Chiun, "Why did you bow to that old fart?"

"It was a gesture of respect."

"You respected him?"

Chiun shrugged. "Only long enough to spit into his tea."

And while Remo was laughing, Chiun turned to General Mefki.

"I seek a carpet merchant named Masood. Do you know of such a man?"

"Yes. Two streets north, and on the right. But do you not have to reach the landing place of these renegades?"

"There is time," said Chiun. "Come, Remo."

As they walked past the blue-tiled mosques, the wailing of the *muezzin* calling the faithful to afternoon prayers filling the dusty air, Remo ventured, "I know what's next."

"Oh?"

"Yep. We're going after the nail. You figure if we present it to the Crusaders, it'll take the wind out of their sails. They won't have any reason to fight."

"Yes, that too."

"Too?"

"After I show you the proper way to purchase a Persian carpet," said Chiun.

The Master of Sinanju strode into the store of the rug merchant Masood Attai.

"I have many rugs, as you can see," Masood Attai said, welcoming them.

"I wish to show my son the proper way to buy a fine carpet," said Chiun. "Observe, Remo." He went over to a stack of rugs nearly three feet tall.

"To detect a rotted warp, you do like so," he said. Taking a corner in both hands, he jerked suddenly. The nap went *snap-pop!*

"I get it," Remo said. "That sound means it's solid. Right?"

"This warp is rotted!" exclaimed Chiun, flaring at the rug merchant.

"You pulled too hard," Masood Attai shot back. "Try this," he said, pulling down a prayer rug hanging on the wall. "This is a fine one," he said, holding it up with difficulty, for it was heavy.

Chiun took it as if it were a mere handkerchief. He examined the nap carefully. He spat on the nap and sniffed the spot.

"Bleached," he said distastefully.

"All moderns are bleached," Masood returned.

Chiun let the rug drop to the floor.

"I do not wish to buy a donkey bag, but a fine Persian carpet. Show me your best."

"Ah," said Masood Attai. He went through a curtain in the rear of the shop and returned lugging a heavy blue rug.

"It is a Ladik. It is very fine. Note the repeating tulips. And for you, only five thousand rials," said Masood Attai as he spread it upon the floor.

While Chiun knelt to examine it, Remo's eyes searched

the shop. He saw the picture of the Ayatollah Khomeini, draped in black. A heavy nail head gleamed dully above it. The portrait hung by a line of frayed string.

Remo's attention drifted back to the Master of Sinanju. Chiun was clucking as he examined the rug's coloring.

"Is this your best?" he asked. "The colors are dull. The rug looks . . . dead."

Masood Attai clapped his old hands. "You are truly a master! I should have recognized this from the start. This is my best rug, but like all moderns, it is woven of *tabachi*, slaughterhouse wool. You are correct that it lacks life. Truly you know rugs. You buy?"

"No!" spat Chiun, rising.

"There is no finer rug woven in this century than that one. What you seek, you must seek from a private collector or a museum. Not from one such as I."

"I am insulted."

"I am sorry. The times have changed."

"You can atone for your insult," suggested Chiun.

"How?"

"That nail. I wish to own it."

Masood Attai looked at the nail suspending the Ayatollah Khomeini's portrait. He spread his hands helplessly.

"I cannot. For I have no other nail. They are scarce now."

"I promise to replace it with a nail you will never lose."

Masood Attai considered. Finally he said, "Done."

And the Master of Sinanju went over to the portrait and lifted it off the nail. He extracted the nail with two delicate fingers. The wooden wall screeched as the nail came out. He tossed the nail to Remo, who caught it with both hands.

Then the Master of Sinanju set the portrait in its proper place with one hand and sent the forefinger of the other hand between the portrait's eyes.

When he withdrew it, the portrait hung perfectly.

Masood Attai screeched. He howled. He swore before Allah that this was a desecration.

"Next time, do not try to sell me a rug with a rotted warp," Chiun called back.

Out on the street, Remo said, "I guess things aren't like they were in the old days."

"I should have known it," Chiun said. "The Moslems have ruined this place."

"I thought Persia was always a Moslem land."

"No. The Arabs ruined it when they took over, bringing their ridiculous religion with them. In truth, Sinanju stopped working for Persia after the great conversion. It is sad. It will pain me to write of this experience in my scrolls."

"Not as much as this will pain you," Remo said slowly. He held up the nail. "Look."

Chiun took the heavy nail. It was almost a spike. It was rusty and dirt-encrusted, but along one flat side of the nail was worn lettering.

It read: *Made in Japan*.

24

Reverend-General Eldon Sluggard descended into the bowels of the *Seaworthy Gargantuan* to address his mighty host. They had passed through the Strait of Hormuz, soon, he hoped, to be rechristened the Strait of Griselda after that other ball-buster, his ex-wife.

Sluggard's heart pounded as he entered the long cargo area. Where viscous brown crude usually sloshed, phalanxes of soldiers in cross-embroidered tunics stood waiting. They were ready. Eldon Sluggard could see it in their feverish eyes.

Reverend-General Sluggard was ready too. He wore two pistols strapped, cowboy style, on his hips. An M16 hung from his shoulder. There were throwing daggers in each boot. And of course his Civil-War-vintage saber, which he was getting used to wearing. He hadn't tripped over it in almost an hour. The sword would be his last line of defense. If it looked like he was going to be captured, he was going to set it hilt-down in the sand and belly-flop onto it. Anything so those ragheads didn't take him alive.

"Ten-hut!" he shouted.

The Paladins of the Lord came to attention. And Reverend-General Sluggard grinned expansively. His grin was as false as a gold tooth, but he knew if he didn't keep them pumped up the mullahs would have him for dinner.

"We are in the Gulf. The Pershing Gulf," he barked.

"Named after that famous American, General John 'Black-jack' Pershing."

"Hallelujah!" they exulted.

"Are we ready to fight?"

"For God and glory!" their voices echoed.

They were nearly six thousand strong. They were young, irrational, and ignorant, but best of all they had an objective. The Holy Nail. Nothing could stand against them.

"We hit the beach in speedboats," said Reverend-General Sluggard. "That way we take 'em by surprise. We establish a beachhead, dig in, and start capturing the oil fields. When we've choked off their economy, we storm our way to Tehran. And the Holy Nail!"

"Hallelujah!"

"The nail is our true objective. All of you remember that the relic of our dear savior's Passion is holding up a picture of the Ayatollah—may he burn in hell."

"Burn!" cried the Hosts of the Lord. Although he had repeated it a dozen times or more, they still broke out in angry indignation every time he reminded them of the nail's fate.

All during the voyage, the Reverend-General had kept churning their emotions. He had told them about what the mullahs were going to do to their Christian family members if they got their way. He told them the story of the original Crusades. They hissed at the story of the First Crusade, which captured, but failed to hold on to Jerusalem. They cheered the story of the successful Third Crusade. They wept and vowed revenge when he told them of the Children's crusade of 1212, when European children sailed into the Holy Land and were captured and made slaves of the heathen.

By the time he had gotten to the Eighth Crusade, they were whipped into a passionate fury. And then he promised them that this would be the Last Crusade. After this, the scourge of the evil Moslems would be eradicated from the world.

"In another minute Ah'm gonna lead you-all up on deck. You know what happens next."

"Victory!"

That wasn't what Eldon Sluggard had in mind, but it sounded good so he went with it.

"Yes! Victory! Victory over Islam. God has called us to a sacred mission and we're gonna accomplish it. And there's one thing I want you to know when we get out there. When all holy hell breaks loose and the bullets are flyin', you remember that bullets are part of the natural world. But you and Ah are part of the spiritual world because we are fortified with the Holy Spirit. And everyone knows that bullets can't touch the Holy Spirit."

"Praise be to the Lord," cried the Paladins of the Lord.

"All right, Reverend-Majors, get your units together! We're going to make Holy War!"

And Reverend-General Sluggard marched topside. The Knights of the Lord followed him in double rows, marching lock-step. He had made them practice the lock-step on the voyage. It was the only military skill he knew. He didn't know beans about guns.

The Persian Gulf air was salty and cool. It was night. A low dark line off the starboard bow was the coast of Iran. It looked foreboding. Here and there lantern-rigged dhows sat on the still water like resting butterflies.

"Start lowering the boats," Reverend-General Eldon Sluggard ordered.

Remo and Chiun arrived at the place marked on the map they had taken from the Christian Campground. It was a tree-covered rise overlooking the Gulf.

"Here," proclaimed Chiun, folding up the map. He slid off the donkey Remo was leading.

"I ride the donkey on the way back," Remo muttered.

"Done," said Chiun. who expected to leave Iran by

ship. They emerged from a clump of olive trees. The water hissed on the sand below.

"Is that the ship?"

Chiun's eyes narrowed. "It says *Seaworthy Gargantuan.* It is the name of the ship we saw departing America."

"Okay, now what do we do? Your great plan is out, unless you think the Crusaders can't read English."

"And I suppose you have a wonderful white plan of your own?" Chiun squeaked.

"Actually not," Remo admitted worriedly. His hearing had picked up sounds, low, disturbing sounds.

Out on the water, a flotilla of speedboats was coming from all directions. They were converging on the *Seaworthy Gargantuan.*

"Revolutionary Guards," Remo said. "They're going for the tanker."

"And land forces too," added Chiun.

Remo turned. Coming up the road were tanks, jeeps, and armored personnel carriers. In the lead was an open jeep, and standing in the back, clutching a copy of the Koran, was the Grand Ayatollah of Iran. Behind him General Mefki's glassy-eyed head bounced. It was perched on the end of a stick.

"Looks like there's been a power struggle with the military," Remo said drily. "Guess who lost."

The vehicles slowed to a halt. The Grand Ayatollah dismounted and walked to a vantage point where he could survey the Gulf.

"*Marg bar Amrika!*" he shouted shaking the Koran over his head. "Let them drown in their own blood."

A screaming horde of Revolutionary Guards poured out of the vehicles. They wore red headbands with revolutionary slogans written on them in white script.

Out in the Gulf, the booming voice of Reverend Sluggard reverberated.

"God is on our side. Let's whip them ragheads!" he shouted.

"Smite them! Allah wills it," returned the Grand Ayatollah.

"You see?" Chiun shouted. "You see, Remo? They call upon the Supreme Creator to aid them in their ridiculous quarrel. Because they call him by different names, fools are willing to go to their deaths."

"So what do we do?"

"You despise the Iranians, do you not?"

"Yeah."

"I make a gift of them to you. I will deal with the Sluggard."

"But—" Remo began. Before he could react, Chiun was running down to the water.

"What the hell," Remo said. He doubled back on the Iranian land force. They were bunched up, exactly counter to all modern rules of close-quarters combat. And they were standing there shouting, "Down, down, USA! Down, down, USA!"

"Up yours!" Remo said, and started to work on them.

On the deck of the *Seaworthy Gargantuan*, Reverend-General Eldon Sluggard saw the speedboats approach.

"While you-all are gettin' into the water," he said, "let me speed you on your way with a few words from the Good Book." He opened his mock Bible and began to recite.

" 'Though Ah walk into the Valley of Death, Ah will fear no Ah-ranian for Ah am the meanest sonovabitch in the valley.' "

"Oh, shut up," Victoria Hoar snapped. She was suddenly beside him. "Get into one of those goddamned boats. You're supposed to be their leader, not their cheerleader."

"Ah'm shoutin' encouragment," he protested. "Ah'll be along once they're rollin'."

Victoria Hoar reached down and pulled one of the throwing knives from Sluggard's own boot. She placed the point at his crotch and warned, "They still make eunuchs in this part of the world. You'd fit right in."

"Ah'm goin'," promised Reverend-General Sluggard.

Then, from across the water, there was a sudden hush. Not even the speedboats could smother it. The hush was momentary. It was followed by a long, low sigh. Then a gasp. Then shouts of "Praise be!"

"What the hell is going on?" Victoria Hoar demanded. She looked out over the water. Her red mouth froze open.

"What the fuck?" said Reverend-General Eldon Sluggard.

For running across the water toward the *Seaworthy Gargantuan* was the Master of Sinanju.

He ran on top of the swells. His sandaled feet made little splashes, but other than that proof of contact with the water he appeared to be floating across the Gulf.

"I do not believe it," Victoria sputtered.

"I told you! I told you!" shouted Eldon Sluggard. "He is the devil, the very devil. He ain't human!"

As everyone watched openmouthed, Chiun sprinted to the hull of the *Seaworthy Gargantuan*. He leapt upon the slippery black hull like a spider. He clung for a moment, then there came a sound like a metal punch going through sheet steel. The sound was repeated. It came again.

Sluggard leaned over the rail.

Below, he saw the old Oriental scaling the hull. With each step, Chiun jammed a finger into the hull. That was what was causing the sound. He used the resulting holes for finger and toe grips.

Eldon Sluggard jumped with each sound.

"Save me! Save me!" he wailed, ducking behind Victoria Hoar. He got down on his knees and blubbered.

"A miracle!" the Paladins of the Lord cried. "It's a sign from Heaven!" They lined the rails to watch, their weapons forgotten.

Chiun came over the rail. His sandals were not even wet.

The Knights of the Lord gathered around him. They sought to touch his robe. They asked for his blessing. The Master of Sinanju evaded their hands even though he was swiftly surrounded. Fingers reached for the hem of his kimono sleeves and it was as if the cloth was insubstantial. Some hands reached out to touch his hands and withdrew, stinging. They never saw the swift, remonstrating blows that made their finger bones go numb.

"I am Chiun."

"Chiun. Great Chiun!" they cried. They shouted his name to the heavens.

Chiun, taken aback, allowed his features to soften.

"Did you say 'great'?" he asked.

"Great Chiun, the messenger of the Lord!" they called.

Chiun smiled. Proper acclaim. This was something new. He raised his open hands as if in blessing.

"I call upon you to cease your war-making," he said.

"It will be done, O Chiun."

"Great Chiun," the Master of Sinanju corrected.

"We have to stop this," Victoria hissed in Sluggard's ear. "He's ruining our whole plan."

"Your whole plan. And I don't want any part of that devil."

"I have an idea. Start reading."

Eldon Sluggard opened his Bible to a random page.

" 'Beware false idols,' " he sang out. " 'For the devil has taken human form to tempt the guillible.' "

He was ignored.

Suddenly Victoria wrenched the book from Sluggard's hands. She presented it to the crowd around Chiun, showing the blank white pages.

"Behold!" she cried. "The pages are blank. The Lord is speaking through his true messenger. It's a miracle!"

"So is walking on water," someone pointed out.

"That's been done before," said Victoria. "This is new."

"Is it truly a miracle?" someone asked. The question was addressed respectfully to the Great Chiun.

"It is a fraud," Chiun replied. "Now I command you to throw away your unnecessary weapons."

His heart sinking, Reverend-General Sluggard watched as the rifles and bayonets and grenades went overboard.

"We're dead," Victoria Hoar said.

"Not me," said Eldon Sluggard. "I'm outta here!" He started to belly over the rail.

"Don't be a fool. Look at those speedboats out there."

"You know that old sayin', better the devil you know than the devil you don't?"

"Yes."

"It don't apply here," said Reverend-General Eldon Sluggard just before he went over the rail. It was a long fall. He hit the water with a huge splash. Sluggard bobbed up on his stomach, facedown, his empty scabbard floating beside him.

A speedboat filled with Revolutionary Guards puttered up and he was pulled from the water. The victorious cries from below indicated that the Iranians recognized the face of their hated enemy Reverend Eldon Sluggard. The speedboat dug in and raced for shore.

On the shore, Remo had routed the Iranians. It was a disappointment. He had hoped to inflict more damage. But as soon as the first few fell with assorted internal injuries, the others turned tail and ran. Remo ran after them. He kicked whirling tires flat. He popped the treads of the decrepit tanks. But the soldiers he pulled out of the ruined vehicles were mostly boys. Few of them looked older than thirteen. Remo hadn't the heart to kill any of them. He sent them on their way with solid kicks to the seats of their khaki pants.

Disgusted, he returned to shore.

On a little hillock, the Grand Ayatollah was shouting imprecations at the Gulf. His bony fists shook with rage. His beard collected spittle from his sphincterlike mouth.

Remo came up from behind and tapped him on the shoulder.

"Hi! Remember me?"

The Grand Ayatollah whirled. His eyes registered shock, then fear as he realized he was alone and with whom.

"Not so brave now?" Remo asked, knowing that the man did not understand English.

"Down, down, USA!" the mullah shouted suddenly, and started off. Remo stepped on the hem of his camelhair robe. The Grand Ayatollah of the Islamic Republic of Iran fell to the ground.

"You know, people said a lot of bad things about the Shah, but you jerks are the pits," Remo said. "I ought to snap your scrawny neck, but my orders are to avoid making this crisis worse than it is."

"Down, down, USA!" the Grand Ayatollah spat. It seemed to be the only English he knew or understood.

"Somewhere I read that the reason you people started this revolution was that the Shah had some of your mullahs' turbans pulled off when they started throwing their weight around. You've caused the world a lot of pain over a damned length of cloth."

And placing a foot on the Grand Ayatollah's heaving chest, Remo took one end of his turban and pulled. The pile of cloth unwound in a twinkling. Remo threw it aside.

"Chiun tells me that was the second worst thing you can do to one of you mullahs. The first is to shave off your beards. Too bad I didn't bring my scissors."

The Grand Ayatollah spat on Remo's loafers.

"Well, what the hell," Remo said. "Anything worth doing is worth doing thoroughly." And he got down on the Grand Ayatollah's chest. He started plucking at the man's beard. With each pluck the Grand Ayatollah howled.

When Remo finally stood up, the Grand Ayatollah was as clean-shaven as a baby's behind.

The Grand Ayatollah, tears erupting from his eyes, screamed his wrath at Remo.

"I don't know what you're saying, pal, but I'm sure the proper response is, 'That's the biz, sweetheart.' "

Remo walked away grinning.

25

Remo Williams saw that the Gulf was quiet. Chiun was standing in the forecastle of the *Seaworthy Gargantuan*, hands tucked into his sleeves. He was addressing Sluggard's disarmed forces. Remo couldn't hear what Chiun was saying, but he noticed that the speedboats of the Revolutionary Guards were standing off the tanker, as if uncertain what to do.

Remo dived into the water and sought them out. He crippled their idling propellers with snapping blows of his hands and then punctured the hulls from below.

The boats sank swiftly. Underwater, Remo reached out for the floundering Revolutionary Guards and pulled them under. He jabbed them in critical areas of the spine, not enough to paralyze them, but to ruin their coordination. If some didn't make it to shore, Remo reasoned, it was not his fault. Just the natural expression of the law of survival of the fittest.

Remo used Chiun's finger holes in the side of *Seaworthy Gargantuan* to reach the deck.

Chiun observed Remo's sopping clothes disdainfully.

"This is my son," he told the crowd. "Remo."

Immediately the Crusaders fell to their knees in supplication.

"The son of the Great Chiun!" they cried. "Great Remo."

"He is not great. He is adequate."

"Adequate Remo," they exulted. "Praise be to Adequate Remo."

Chiun turned to Remo.

"Now do you understand?" he whispered. "This is how these things begin. These people will go back to their homes and tell of Chiun the Great and the Adequate Remo. They will start churches. They will make up rules to keep their followers in line, and in a mere three or four centuries, we will be considered deities ourselves."

Remo saw the worshipful gazes being directed at him. They reminded him of the expression on his own face when he was with Reverend Sluggard's ministry. Their sheeplike acceptance disgusted him.

"You've made your point," Remo said quietly.

"It is ridiculous. It is wrong."

"I said you made your point," Remo repeated testily.

"Let us give tribute to the Great Chiun." This from a kneeling member of the crowd.

"We have had enough of your tribute," Chiun began to say.

But when the coins and paper money, not to mention whole wallets, began falling at his sandaled feet, Chiun whispered to Remo, "Do not just stand there. Help me collect my rightful tribute from these proper worshipers of perfection."

"You can't take money from them under false pretenses, Little Father," Remo said. "It's wrong."

"And it is a long boat ride home. We must keep these cretins in line. And what better way to do it than this? Besides, if they are so deluded that they take me for a higher being, how is that my mistake?"

"Tell you what, you take care of this. I'll handle Sluggard and Victoria. Where are they?"

"I do not know," Chiun said, tearing open a fat wallet. He threw the identification cards and the credit cards overboard and stuffed the money into a secret pocket in his kimono.

"The Iranians got Reverend Sluggard," said a pimplefaced Crusader. He pointed toward the coastline.

A speedboat had slowed in the water. Revolutionary Guards were wading ashore. They carried the limp bloated body of Reverend Eldon Sluggard like a fat pig being hoisted to a feast.

Remo's first impulse was to go after Sluggard. He hesitated at the rail. Then he said, "Screw him. He's not worth it. That just leaves Victoria."

Remo searched the ship. He found Victoria Hoar on the captain's bridge, high in the white superstructure. Victoria was giving orders to the captain.

"You listen to me. We've got to dump these people. They're all witnesses to the company's involvement. Get us out to the open sea, and we'll herd them into a flood-control compartment and let the water in. We can dump the bodies on the way home."

"Not a very Christian attitude," Remo said coolly.

Victoria Hoar turned suddenly. Remo was leaning across the doorjamb. He stood on one leg, the other crossed over it. His bare arms were folded.

"Remo!"

"Why don't you excuse us," Remo told the captain.

"You are not the master of this vessel," the captain protested.

Remo changed the captain's mind. He knocked out a window and dangled him out of it. When he felt the captain secure a handhold, he let go. The captain scrambled down the superstructure like a frightened monkey.

"Sluggard's in Iranian hands," Remo said quietly.

"For him that's a fate worse than death. But he deserved it, the idiot."

"I gather from what I overheard that you're the real brain behind this. Right?"

Victoria Hoar dug out a cigarette and lit it. She exhaled smoke slowly.

"Yes. He hadn't the brains of a gnat. But he had a gift and I knew how to control him. I suppose you have a lot of obvious questions."

"Yeah."

"You know it wasn't over the nail," she went on, nervously pacing the bridge. "That was just a device. I spotted the nail on a trip to Tehran. It's a fake. Even Sluggard didn't believe it was the true nail. I was desperate to get my company back in the black. When I first saw the nail, the whole scheme came to me in a flash. Divine inspiration, you might say. All I needed was the right front man. Sluggard was my first choice. He was perfect."

"I know. Chiun has the nail. It says 'Made in Japan' on it."

Victoria Hoar blew out a little laugh with her smoke.

"It could have worked. With enough Crusaders, we could have gained control of the oil fields. The damned war had sapped Iran of fighting men so badly, they were an easy mark. Believe it or not, we could have taken over. If not this time, then next."

"Maybe. But not without breaking a lot of eggs."

"Excuse me?"

"Your cannon fodder. You can't make an omelet without breaking a few eggs."

Victoria Hoar shrugged. "I didn't invent testosterone. I just know how to harness it. So what's next? Do you surrender me to the authorities?"

"We don't work that way."

"And who's we?"

"The fact that you know that there is a 'we' makes you a liability."

Victoria Hoar blinked. She looked at Remo's face. It was hard. The mouth, unsmiling, looked cruel. Even the eyes, which back in Thunderbolt had been so guileless, were now deep and pitiless. He was a different Remo now. But he was still a man. And all men respond to one thing. She stubbed out her cigarette and stepped up to him. She tugged at his belt buckle, a friendly, playful tug.

"You won't kill me," she breathed.

"Why not?" Remo said, looking her in the eyes. Her

hands were straying toward his zipper. Her breath, once sweet, smelled of tobacco smoke. Remo hadn't known she was a smoker.

"Because I know you. You wouldn't kill a lady."

Her mouth parted. Her lips rose to meet his. Remo felt them brush his own. Her tongue touched his lightly, playfully.

"You're right," Remo said, drawing back. "I wouldn't kill a lady."

Victoria Hoar smiled. She had judged him right. Her fingers started to pull down his zipper.

"For a while I was doubting myself," Remo said quietly. "I thought my work, the things I had to do, were wrong. But now I see a greater wrong. Not doing my job."

Remo reached up to brush a lock of hair back from her smooth white neck, as if to kiss it. But instead of his lips, Victoria Hoar felt his forefinger and thumb bear down on her carotid artery. His fingers felt strong. She shivered with the anticipation of their caress. But no caress was coming. The fingers stayed firm and Victoria Hoar felt the darkness edging in at the periphery of her vision. And she knew that she would never feel Remo's caress—or any man's caress—ever again.

"Better that I take care of the likes of you and Sluggard than sit on my hands while you screw up the world."

"But you said—" Victoria started to say.

"You're no lady," Remo said, clamping hard.

Victoria Hoar made a clumsy pile of arms and legs on the bridge floor. There was nothing sexy about her anymore.

Remo walked away without a backward glance.

Reverend Eldon Sluggard woke up painfully. It was dark. His hands hit something hard and metallic and he said, "Ouch!"

He pulled himself up on one elbow and looked around.

He recognized that he was lying on the floor of an armored personnel carrier. It was like being inside one of the armored cars that carried donations to his bank, except instead of money he was surrounded by evilly grinning Iranians.

Their too-white teeth were directed at him.

Reverend Sluggard felt for his sidearm holsters. They were empty. His scabbard was full of seawater, but that was all. He pulled himself up into a seated position. He grinned back.

"Hi!" he said. He reached for his left boot, where there was a throwing dagger. But it was empty too. Then he remembered that the bitch had it.

That still left the right boot. All it contained was his soggy foot. The frozen grin on the Reverend Eldon Sluggard's face collapsed.

"Where we goin'?" he croaked.

"To Tehran. You will like it there. Everyone will wish to meet you. Everyone." Those grins got even wider, if that was possible. There was something familiar about them. He put his finger on it after a while. He had seen those grins in his nightmares, the perfect ivory teeth, the wickedly gleaming eyes. They belonged to the devil. And then it hit him that he was in a land of devils.

"Say," asked the Reverend Eldon Sluggard suddenly, "have you boys heard about Jesus?"

26

Dr. Harold W. Smith knocked on the door.

"Come in," Remo Williams called.

Smith found Remo rolling up his reed sleeping mat. A blue toothbrush stuck out of a chino pocket.

"What are you doing?" Smith asked.

"Packing," Remo said.

"Trip?"

"No. Chiun and I have come to a decision. We're moving out of this lunatic asylum. No offense, but that's what Folcroft is."

"None taken," Smith said. "And that is probably just as well. I have been hinting to Chiun that you've been here too long."

"This isn't Chiun's idea. It's mine. Chiun likes it here. He thinks the royal assassin should live in-house, so to speak. But he's agreed to come with me."

"That is nice of him. Unusually nice."

"He's still pretty shaken over our trip to Iran. It was bad enough the melons sucked and the rugs were all inferior, but the high-mucky-muck mullah had never heard of Sinanju. Worse, he was terrified of America. Chiun still can't figure that one out. I don't think we'll ever hear him threaten to quit America for Persia again. And speaking of that assignment, are all the dangling ends tied up?"

"As best we can do. The Crusaders have been returned to their families. The government has decided not to bring action against Mammoth Oil and Shale for violations of the Neutrality Act, largely because they're about to go under financially. And as far as Iran's public statements about American attempts to invade their nation go, they've been crying wolf for so long no one else in the international community takes their claims seriously."

"What about the Crusaders who died in the first wave?"

"The Booe boy's death, although at the hands of Iranians, occurred at Sluggard's ministry. That makes it liable. I imagine there will be a handsome settlement for the boy's family. As far as the others go, the Iranians show no sign of relinquishing those bodies. I'm afraid they're going to join the ranks of the permanently missing unless something comes out of the flood of lawsuits about to descend upon the Sluggard organization. Given the state of our court system, there may be a friendly regime in Iran by then."

"I like a happy ending," Remo said wryly. "By the way, I've been meaning to ask. How did you crack that terrorist at FBI headquarters?"

Smith looked at his feet. "It was nothing," he said uncomfortably.

"Smitty! You're embarrassed. Come on, let's hear it."

Smith cleared his throat. "As you know, it takes three days to crack an interrogation subject. We didn't have that much time. I used a technique I had once employed when I was with the OSS and needed information from an Axis collaborator caught after he had betrayed the hiding place of a number of Jewish refugees to the Nazis."

"Go on. I'm enthralled."

"Er, I talked to him."

"Talked?"

"Calmly and collectedly. I did not accuse or harangue either man regarding his crimes. Instead, I spoke quietly of the people whose deaths they had caused. I read them intimate details about their lives. I showed photographs. I spoke of the grief of their loved ones. In short, I put faces on what had been faceless victims. The terrorist broke when I laid a photo of a seven-year-old girl he had killed on the table and read to him from a class assignment she had written the previous week. It was entitled, 'What I Want To Be When I Grow Up.' When I read the portion describing how the girl wanted to become a nurse and end human suffering, the man broke like a soap bubble."

"Knowing you, Smitty, you probably bored him to death. Either way, it was pretty neat. Congratulations."

"Um, thank you."

At that moment the Master of Sinanju walked in.

"Greetings, Emperor Smith," he said stiffly. He had not entirely forgiven Smith for his earlier transgressions against his pride. "Has my son broken the bitter news to you?"

"Yes, Master Chiun. And this is excellent timing. I just received your steamer trunks."

"Good. We recovered them from Sluggard's yacht before departing for Per—Iran. I warned the PUS man that it would be his head if they were not treated with proper respect."

"UPS man," said Smith.

"All fourteen have arrived?"

"All fourteen."

"No broken locks or damaged panels?"

"They appear to be in good condition."

"Well, if that's that," Remo said brightly, "let's go."

"Have you a place to stay?" asked Smith.

"Chiun and I are thinking of buying a house."

"Well, I can't stop you. But I must caution against a permanent address. Security, you understand."

"Caution away. But we're buying a house. With a white picket fence. And maybe a garden."

"With melons," added Chiun.

"Let me know the instant you pass papers," Smith said.

"Don't worry, Smitty. We'll be sending you the bill. You coming, Chiun?"

"One moment, Remo. I must confer with my emperor. Please be so good as to check my trunks for damage."

"Gotcha," said Remo, skipping down the hall.

"He appears to be very happy," Smith remarked quietly.

"He will get over it. Remo's happiness has always been as fleeting as the spring snows."

"Does this have anything to do with his recent religious awakening?"

"No, Remo's religious reawakening was like his moods. When it was strong, it filled the room. I do not know what brought it on, but Reverend Sluggard's false words put it back to sleep."

"That is probably for the best. In our line of work there is no room for spiritual questioning."

"Besides, I have instructed him in the Sinanju beliefs," Chiun said proudly. "All vestiges of his old religion, the names of gods and the superstitions, have been purged from his mind."

At that moment Remo poked his head in. "Hey, Chiun what's the holdup? Jesus, Mary, and Joseph. Shake a leg, will ya!"

"Then again," Chiun said darkly, "what can you do with someone after the Church of Rome has had him for his first twenty summers?"